PROTECTING HER *Heart*

BOOK 3

 HEALING HEARTS
A *Lesbian Medical Romance* Drama Series

MT CASSEN

Read the first half of Melody in Her Heart now!

"What Do You Do If Your Mind Can't Understand But Your Heart Can't Let Go?"

CHAPTER ONE

Bella

The halls of Capmed were filled with people running every which way, giving Bella Strong a bad case of nerves. Her heart raced, and she scanned her eyes in several directions. Did she know what she was truly getting herself into?

She put on a wide smile and approached the registration desk. "Name and reason you need to be seen?" the woman at the desk asked, barely looking up to make eye contact.

"Hi, I'm Bella Strong. I have an appointment with Margo Smythe. She's with the—"

"Hold on, please," the woman said. She swiveled her chair away from Bella and turned to her phone.

Bella snapped her mouth shut and waited for her to come back around. She was currently in the last semester of her university's nursing program and working at Capmed was the next step in her life plan. Bella ran through her plan in her head again, as if she

1

hadn't done it a million times before. Graduate at twenty-two. Get a full-time nursing job at Capmed. Marry Jackson. Start a family. And it all needed to happen before she turned thirty.

The woman turned around, her eyes refocusing on her computer. "Take hallway E down until it T's, then take a right, followed by another right. She's in office number one-four-two."

"Hallway E?" Bella asked. Her voice trembled slightly. Now wasn't the time to break. She was about to have her first day, and if she faltered too many times, they would laugh her right out of the hospital.

The woman looked up and gave a weak smile. "Right behind me. It's labeled E. At the end of the hallway, take a right, followed by another right. And then…"

"Office one-four-five," Bella completed for her.

The woman glanced up at her with a frown. "No. One-four-two. She'll be waiting for you."

Bella swallowed at her blunder. "Got it. Thank you very much!" Bella exclaimed.

She turned and released a breath. She could do this. She was born to be a nurse, just like her mom, and she was ready to prove that to her family—but most importantly, to herself.

———

As Bella walked toward Margo's office, she recalled how she had met the woman. Her sister Veronica's best friend, Brittany, just happened to be the daughter of Tabby, one of the nurses at Capmed. When Veronica had mentioned that Bella was in her last semester going for her bachelor's in nursing, Tabby had seemed enthusiastic and had mentioned a new program that she had helped develop at Capmed. The rest was history. Now, Bella was about to meet Margo, the woman who could give Bella the opportunity she was looking for. She prayed she wasn't making the wrong jump in her career. But Capmed was an amazing hospital, so it must be the right choice.

Bella followed the path to the office, just as the woman behind the reception desk had laid out to her. When she reached Margo's door, she exhaled and knocked.

"Enter," a woman's voice hollered.

Here goes nothing. Bella entered the office, prepared to release any negative feelings and make the best impression she could. What she hadn't anticipated was immediately being thrown into the fire as Margo took her up to the pediatrics ward without so much as a welcome or any other information.

"This is Dr. Whalen," Margo said, motioning to a man standing at the receptionist's desk as she made her introductions. "I think we'll have you round with him." She held up her hand to shield her mouth before she added, "His bark is way worse than his bite."

"I heard that," he responded, his voice booming out from underneath his mustache.

Bella smiled at the gleam in his eye. "I'm Bella Strong. It's a pleasure to meet you, Dr. Whalen," she said.

"The pleasure is all mine. Now, Margo, if you'll leave this young protégée to me, I'll have her working the halls of this hospital like a pro."

Margo smirked. "I have all the confidence you will." She reached out and touched Bella's arm. "It was nice to meet you. Know that we are one big family, and you are going to excel here." She winked at Bella, then turned and left.

It was nice to hear those words, and they put Bella at greater ease.

"Follow me," Dr. Whalen said. He started walking away, and Bella hurried to keep up. She couldn't be known as a dawdler or straggler. She had to make sure he saw that she was putting in all the effort she could muster.

They approached a woman. "Ms. Strong," Dr. Whalen started.

"Bella," she quickly interrupted. "Just Bella."

He nodded. "All right, Bella. This is Tori Mitchell, and she's one of the lead nurses on this floor. If you can't find me, you go to her. If you can't find her…" He hesitated. "Then send out the troops because we're all in a heap of trouble."

Tori laughed. "He makes jokes. That's why we keep him around." Tori reached up and touched his arm, and he gave a gentle chuckle.

Bella had to remind herself that Margo did say Dr. Whalen's bark was worse than his bite. As far as she could see, he was just a giant teddy bear—maybe even the papa of the floor. She made a mental note, anticipating that he would also be the one she frequently reported to. After all, he did mention that. Right?

Bella grimaced to herself. She had a notebook full of notes that she had taken during orientation and studied up on, but what with the fast-paced nature of Capmed, Bella worried she wouldn't be able to keep up.

Bella's stomach churned. This position was something that could either make or break her. If she could keep up with the accelerated BSN program, she could have a secure job by the end of it. If she couldn't handle studying and working, she would be a major failure and her entire plan would be thrown off. And then what? She'd be a nobody, which is exactly what her high school bullies had told her she'd be. She had been a little awkward back then and had struggled with her grades, but she was so much better now. She *had* failed one class in her first semester of undergrad, but she'd been working her butt off since then, and everything had been fine. She was on the path to a wonderful, successful life, to proving all of her old peers wrong. She wasn't a screw-up. She could do this.

She only needed to avoid having a panic attack on her first day.

Tori had a frozen smile on her face, waiting for Bella to respond. "Um, hi," Bella said, snapping out of her inner spiral. "It's nice to meet you, Tori."

She nodded. "Same to you. Good luck around here."

Before Bella could walk away, Tori said, "Oh, and just so you know..." She reached across the desk and held up a folder as if it were a trophy. "You'll want to get accustomed to this folder. This is where you'll find all your information about what rotation you're on. But don't worry about all that. It'll gradually come to you."

Bella nodded. "Thank you!"

Another thing to go on in that notebook of hers. Should she bring it to work and carry it around to refer to and take notes, or would that be seen as a weakness? She certainly didn't want to give her coworkers the wrong impression, like she wasn't capable. But what if she forgot something important and they told her to leave?

No. That wouldn't happen. She'd remember everything, and she had the folder Tori gave her for help.

Fifteen minutes down and just eight more hours to go. She could do this. She already was. She hoped.

———

BELLA'S CELLPHONE RANG, AND SHE GROANED. IT WAS THE way Dr. Whalen said he could best reach his nurses. What she didn't account for was the fact that he needed to reach his nurses every fifteen minutes. She grabbed her phone from her pocket and answered it. "Hello, Dr. Whalen."

"Four-zero-six needs meds. The script was written on his chart. And four-one-two needs his vitals taken."

"All right, I'm on it," she said, hoping her voice came across as chipper.

Bella stifled a yawn as she disconnected the call, then checked her watch. She groaned. It was already nearly three o'clock in the morning, and she had intended on getting out of there by two. She had a test at eight and would need to get up no later than six to freshen up. She hadn't prepared herself for this part of her responsibilities.

She retrieved her patient's medication from the automated dispenser and delivered it to room four-zero-six with a cup of water. Then, Bella quietly stepped into the other patient's room to get a full set of vital signs. By the time she had everything documented, it was almost three-thirty. She grabbed her phone from her pocket and stared at it. Just like clockwork, it started to ring.

"Hello, Dr. Whalen." She released a breath, then inhaled and held it, waiting for him to rattle off another list of patients who needed her assistance. She was exhausted, and surely these pediatric patients could hold off until later in the morning when another nurse came in.

"Just noticed the time. You should get out of here. Job well done, though. See you next time. Make sure you check the schedule on your way out." Bella opened her mouth to inquire about that, but Dr. Whalen beat her to it. "It's in the folder that Tori showed you when you first got here."

"Ah, thank you, Dr. Whalen. See you later."

Bella had given her class schedule to Capmed, so she was hopeful whoever was responsible for her schedule didn't mess anything up. When she checked the folder, she was relieved to see that her schedule did fit around her schoolwork, though it didn't give much time beyond that. She took a picture of it and shrugged. It was what it was. This wasn't going to be forever. Only four more months and she would be finished with school. She'd be able to stop the juggling act and focus solely on work. She only needed to survive until then.

Her stomach twisted. *Could* she survive until then? She had to, or the ideal life she'd designed for herself would be ruined.

Bella hurried to the locker room and grabbed her purse and bag, then left the hospital as quickly as she could. The sooner she got home to her apartment, the better chance she would get to fall asleep and have at least some time to relax before she had to get up for her classes.

The good thing about working into the morning hours was missing all the traffic, and Bella made it home in record time. She collapsed into her bed, not even bothering to get out of her scrubs. It felt like no sooner had she closed her eyes than her alarm went off.

"This can't be right," she mumbled.

She opened her eyes and looked over at her clock. Sure enough, six o'clock flashed on the LED screen. She reached over and shut the alarm off, then fell back in bed and stared up at the ceiling. Somehow, her eyes closed, and by the time she opened them again, they were looking at a clock that read seven-thirty.

"Crap," she cried.

Bella jumped up from her bed and worked double-time to shower and get dressed. She had her hair pulled up into a messy bun and was out the door with only a granola bar in fifteen minutes. Still, even that didn't get her to her campus on time. She rushed into the classroom fifteen minutes late.

Immediately, Professor Julian looked over and stared at her. The whole class remained quiet, and Bella felt her cheeks grow instantly hot.

"So glad you decided to join us today, Ms. Strong," he said in his heavy Italian accent.

"Sorry for the interruption," she mumbled. She moved in,

brushing past a chair that made a loud screech across the floor. She paused as students giggled all around her. She wanted to crawl into a hole and never be seen again, but she had to carefully maneuver her way up the bleacher steps to reach an empty seat. She fumbled with her bag as it clumsily fell to the floor, making another loud noise echo through the auditorium room. *Shoot me now.*

She looked up and met her professor's gaze, as he hadn't said a word the whole time she was fumbling her way to her seat. "Are you ready?" he asked dryly.

She nodded, a yawn escaping her, which caused her to squeak in embarrassment and him to arch an eyebrow in her direction. "Sorry," she whispered, covering her mouth.

"Where was I before the interruption?" the professor asked.

Hands shot up all around her, as the rest of the class was eager to impress. Bella rolled her eyes and pulled out the required textbook for her accounting class. She just wanted the class to be over, but more importantly, she wanted to make sure she didn't nod off to sleep. That was the last thing she needed in a day that had already started horribly.

What was wrong with her? Was she slipping back into the high school girl she'd fought so hard to change? If she kept this up, she'd fail her last semester, which would set her back. Then she wouldn't get married by twenty-five and have kids by thirty. What would she be then? A failure, that's what.

The day had to get better. Her life had to get easier. She had to prove to herself and everyone else that she could do whatever she set out to do and that she *was* capable. Otherwise, what good was she?

CHAPTER TWO

Bella

The restaurant was busy when Bella entered and glanced around for Jackson. When she saw him, she smiled, her worries and awful morning washing away. He was the only person she looked at as she approached him.

He pulled her into his arms and murmured, "Good afternoon, beautiful."

"Good afternoon," she replied, squirming a little. She didn't like when he called her beautiful. It wasn't because of any low self-esteem; it just never made her melt when he said it. He was her boyfriend, though, so she needed to get more comfortable with him calling her that.

She smiled, finally able to take a small break. She was no longer exhausted as she sat down across from him in the corner booth. He gave her second wind, and her morning of being late and belittled by her professor was instantly forgotten.

"I needed to lunch with you," she said, grabbing her glass of water and taking a sip, then sighing.

He tilted his head. "That's obvious from the way you're looking. You seem a little frazzled."

She reached up and touched her messy bun, grimacing when she felt that half her hair had already fallen out of the elastic band.

She cringed. "I probably look like a mess."

He reached out and grabbed her hand, offering her a wink. "Babe, you look beautiful. Just saying that I can tell when my honey is stressing."

Bella nodded. "And I absolutely am." She leaned forward and flipped her menu open and looked through it. "We can discuss that later. Have you decided what you're going to order?"

"Chicken and pasta sound good," Jackson offered.

Bella smiled and looked up. "I'm good with that."

As if on cue, the waitress approached them and turned her attention to Bella. "My name is Jess and I'll be taking your order. Do you want anything besides water?"

"Water is fine. Thanks," Bella said. "And I do believe we're ready to order." She motioned to Jackson, and he placed their order. Then the waitress was gone, and Bella closed her eyes. "Where to begin," she started.

"The beginning is always a good start," Jackson replied.

When she opened her eyes, she saw that he had a hint of a glimmer in his eyes. She smiled. He knew her better than any other person did. They had met in the jewelry store he owned. She was there to get a bracelet clasp replaced from a bracelet she had inherited from her grandmother. He had fixed it easily while explaining that he had taken over his father's jewelry shop and came from a long line of jewelry makers. He intrigued her, and they had developed a solid friendship. When he said he had feelings and wanted something more, she decided it was perfect timing. He was a good guy and would make a good father, and she cared for him. They didn't have a passionate relationship, but it was enough. And she no longer needed to date because Jackson fit into her life plan.

It also helped that her parents loved him. So why not choose Jackson?

They had developed a solid bond over the past two years, and he hadn't been fazed when she told him about her plan. He had agreed that she needed to get her degree and secure a great nursing job, and then they would marry and have at least one kid by her thirtieth birthday.

As Bella told him about being late to her first class, he listened intently. His eyes were focused on her, and he seemed completely zoned in on every word she had to say. There wasn't any indication that he was judging her. She liked that about him.

"Everyone's late at some point. It just happens. I'm sure your professor doesn't blame you for that."

Bella smirked and sipped her water. "Spoken by someone who doesn't know Professor Julian. His eyes can bear daggers into a person's soul."

Jackson laughed and shook his head. "Well, if that's how he is, then I would say who needs him. You'll be finished with this class in a few months and be able to look back and sigh with relief."

At that moment, Jess returned with their food. "Thank you," Bella replied, quickly digging in. She munched on her meal and nodded. "You are so right."

He smiled. "That's what I like to see. That beautiful smile on your lips."

She nodded, ignoring how his words didn't cause butterflies—or anything at all. She looked down at her food and took another bite. "Pretty good," she said, wiping her mouth and then taking a sip of her water.

"So, how was your first night at the hospital? I was worried about you. It seemed like too much, getting off so late and then having to head to class."

"You don't even know the half of it," she mumbled. "I got out late and might as well have only had an hour to sleep. By the time I had unwound and closed my eyes, my alarm was already going off."

Bella shook her head, thinking back to earlier that morning. It was overwhelming, but somehow it brought a feeling of exhilaration inside of her. A few more nights like that and she was sure she would get used to it.

Jackson listened as she dished on her experience working at the hospital, and when she was done, he tilted his head. "And this is a part-time gig, right? Don't want you overstretching yourself."

She smiled. "Thank you. You're always so sweet to me."

He reached out and brushed his hand against her cheek. "Well, I love you."

"Me, too," she responded. She'd never been able to get the L-word out for Jackson, but love wasn't necessary to have a good life and relationship. They had mutual respect, and she cared for him. They made a good team.

"I won't overstretch, I promise," she continued. "I'm going to enjoy it. Sure, it's going to be a lot, but I didn't expect this to be easy. Nothing worthwhile ever is, right?"

He shook his head. "You always amaze me, babe."

As Bella opened her mouth to respond, her phone started ringing. She reached into her purse and saw *Capmed* spread across the screen. She looked up and gave him a sheepish grin.

"Speaking of…" She held up the phone to show him the name that was flashing on the screen. He arched his brow as she answered the call. "This is Bella."

"Hello, Bella. This is Tori Mitchell. We met late last night. I'm the lead nurse in the pediatrics department."

"Of course," Bella said. "I remember."

"Perfect. Anyway, there was a call-in for this evening. I know that you had a late one last night, but I checked your school schedule, and it seems you only had morning classes today. I was hoping you could come in tonight. It would only be for a few hours. Five or six tops."

Bella shook her head in disbelief. *She called that a few?*

"Um, well…" She hesitated, glancing across the table at Jackson's expectant stare.

"You would be helping me out greatly. I understand if you're not free, but I'm kind of in a bind here."

Tori hesitated a bit before continuing. "I know this kind of puts you on the spot, and technically you're only a nursing assistant, but this will look great on your resume, whether you choose to stay with Capmed or go somewhere else." She laughed on the other end of the line. "I'm begging you here. We had two more pediatric patients come in this morning, and we're stretched thin."

"You don't have to beg, Tori. I'll be there in twenty minutes."

"Really?" she squealed. "Thank you so much!"

"My pleasure." Bella disconnected the call, and Jackson's jaw dropped.

"Babe, you're exhausted."

"I'll get some sleep," Bella argued, standing. She saw Jackson's gaze drop to her half-eaten food. "I'll finish this during a break."

She waved Jess over to the table. "Can I please get a to-go box?"

Jess quickly left and returned a moment later with a box in her hands.

"Thank you." Bella packed her food and looked up to find

Jackson's eyes still on her. "Listen, the more I help them out, the more they'll be willing to help me out, right?"

"I suppose," he mumbled. "Just don't overexert yourself. That won't be good for anyone."

Bella leaned in and kissed his cheek. "I won't. I'll call you later." She turned with her food in her hands, then looked over her shoulder. "Thanks for lunch." She held up her box, then hurried out of the restaurant. She had to get to the hospital and start her second shift, whether her body was ready or not.

———

As Bella approached Tori, the lead nurse looked up. Tori's hair was a mess and a smidge of her blush had streaked on her face. She sighed and practically collapsed into a chair across from Bella.

"I'm so glad you could come in. You have no idea how much I appreciate this."

Bella put on a wide grin. "Happy to help."

She glanced over to where a woman had just exited a room with Dr. Whalen. Bella couldn't help but stare. The woman was stunning and oozed confidence. She looked to be completely in her element, waving to a nearby nurse. Though she was just wearing a lab coat and scrubs, she had an elegance that stole Bella's breath.

She pulled her eyes away so she wouldn't be caught gawking. She looked at Tori, motioning to the woman and trying to seem disinterested. "Who's that?"

Tori looked, following her gaze, then smiled. "Oh, that? That's Dr. Leona Guillano. She just transferred here from New York City." Tori handed a folder to her. "And your next patient is waiting in his room. He needs fluids and is in major need of some rest. He was brought here from Indianapolis this morning. Six years old."

She started rattling off other information, then smiled. "You've got this. Same drill from before. Dr. Whalen couldn't praise you enough."

Bella looked up from the chart and arched an eyebrow. "Really?"

"Yep." Tori got up from the computer and grabbed another chart. "Said you were on top of things. That's high praise for him." She laughed. "Anyway, best get to it. No rest for the weary."

She started to leave, then snapped her fingers and spun on her heel. "Almost forgot—Karen won't be in until six. I hope you don't mind staying. And I'll be out of here in an hour."

Bella's jaw dropped. What happened to only a few hours?

"You're a lifesaver," Tori added. She turned and entered a room, accidentally knocking Bella back in the process.

She shook her head. She hadn't even gotten a chance to argue against it. It was like Tori had this way of making Bella feel like it was her idea to stick around three hours longer than intended. She chewed her bottom lip and looked down at her chart, checking the room number. What had she gotten herself into?

Before heading to her patient—Brad, the chart said—she glanced around for Dr. Guillano, but the woman had disappeared. It was strange how drawn Bella was to this doctor. She shook the thought from her head. She was tired, and the doctor was beautiful. That was all.

She knocked on Brad's door, waiting for someone to welcome her in. When she didn't hear anything, she knocked a little louder. "Hello? May I come in?" she asked, peering her head through the door.

"Come in!" Brad looked up from his book.

Bella looked around the room, expecting that a mom or dad

would be just a couple of feet away. Instead, the kid was alone. She turned back to him, noticing his wide brown eyes.

"Hello," he said, his voice chipper.

"Why, hello there." Bella grabbed her stool and pulled up next to him. "Are you Brad Carver?" she asked.

He nodded, his cheeks rosy and his eyes bright. He then leaned forward and coughed hard, choking as he fell back onto his pillow. Bella jumped up and grabbed him his glass of water, then helped him take a few sips.

"Are you okay?" she asked.

He looked up, tears leaking from the corners of his eyes. He nodded. "The doctors said I have a virus. But the doctors here are the best. That's what they told me."

"Who's 'they'?" Bella asked, taking her seat back on the stool.

"Kimberly Blackstone."

Bella swiveled her chair at the sound of a woman's voice. The woman in question wore a black pinstripe skirt and blouse, and she walked with purpose. Her tanned features were almost as dark as her jet-black hair that cascaded over her shoulders.

"Hello," Bella said, shaking the woman's offered hand. "And you are…"

"I work at Chesterhill Children's Home in Indianapolis. I'm sorry I was away, but Brad is one of two kids I have here."

Children's home? At least that explained why there wasn't a mother or father by Brad's side.

"Nice to make your acquaintance. I'm Bella Strong, the nurse who's been assigned on Brad's rotation this afternoon."

Kimberly nodded. "So, what's the verdict? We hear it's 'just' a virus, but since Melody Jane had to come here for her cancer treatment, I thought I would get Brad checked out."

"Well, it could very well be just a virus. Dr. Whalen will be coming in shortly and will make sure to get Brad all checked out. I see some of Brad's symptoms are fever, cough, upset stomach, and tremors. Anything else to note?"

Kimberly shook her head. "That just about covers it," she said.

"I've been monitoring his BP, and it seems normal. His pulse is a bit elevated, but nothing too erratic to worry about." Bella turned to face the boy and grabbed her thermometer. "Let me get your temp. Open your mouth."

She slipped the thermometer under Brad's tongue and waited for it to beep before checking it and nodding. "One hundred point five. A little higher than I'd like, so I'll get him some aceta-minophen."

She stood up from his stool and frowned. There was something else she was supposed to do, right? She thought she had recalled Tori mentioning something, but she skimmed over the chart and shrugged. "I'll let the doctor know you're ready and get you that medicine to cut the fever."

"Thank you," Kimberly said.

Bella left the room and went over to the medicine cabinet. She measured out the appropriate dose of acetaminophen and docu-mented the release of medicine on the cabinet, just as she was shown the night before. At least she had remembered this impor-tant step. Little by little, she was getting the hang of things, but she still felt so slow and not on top of things as she normally was. What if she couldn't do this job?

She pushed those thoughts away as she carried the cup back into Brad's room. "Go ahead and drink this all up. Here's some water to wash it down. The doctor will be in with you in just a few minutes. Until then, I'll be right outside these doors if you need me."

"Thank you," Brad said before lying back against his pillow.

"You are very welcome. Feel better soon."

She turned and left his room. Bella looked up and down the

hallway, waiting for Dr. Whalen to come out of one of the hospital rooms. Instead, it was the new doctor, Dr. Guillano, who emerged, heading straight toward Bella. She had her hair pulled back into a ponytail, giving her a younger look, although Bella would guess she was in her mid-forties. She didn't have wrinkles to prove that, but the way she moved when she walked showed she had years on Bella. Her stature was one of independence and maturity, not like the awkward girl Bella sometimes felt she portrayed.

"Is that chart for me?" the doctor asked, approaching her.

Bella realized she had been gawking, lost in the woman's eyes. Bella looked away. "Uh, I mean, um..." Bella swallowed and looked over the chart. "Um, it should be for Dr. Whalen."

Dr. Leona Guillano frowned. "It's not Brad Carver?" she asked.

Bella's insides tensed. It was, but she was supposed to be working with Dr. Whalen. That's how things were done, right? Work with the same doctor repetitively, so you would get used to how they operated. She chewed her lip. She was so confused.

"It is, but..." Her words trailed off when Leona grabbed the chart and smiled.

"Yep. It's mine." She started to turn but stopped herself and looked over her shoulder. "Silly me. I'm Dr. Leona Guillano. I believe you'll be working with me this shift."

She grabbed a piece of paper from her pocket and held it up to show it to Bella. Bella's name was written underneath the doctor's. Dr. Guillano smiled. "The patient in room four-zero-two needs an extra blanket."

"Yes, ma'am," Bella replied, still in slight shock.

Dr. Guillano turned and headed to Brad's room, leaving Bella in her dust. There was a hurried tone in her words, but a small smile showed on her lips. It made her a woman first, a doctor second. She didn't look much like the doctors Bella had met. She had dimples that touched the corners of her smile, and she wore makeup, even though it was lightly done. But she had this way about her that got people's attention. Maybe it was her stride. Or maybe it was the way her eyes homed in on Bella that made her feel seen. Being in Dr. Guillano's presence also gave her a warm sensation in her core, something she'd never felt with Jackson or with anyone else.

She sighed. She needed to ignore whatever crazy things were happening in her body because of this doctor. The last thing she needed was to develop a crush when she was already struggling with work and school. Besides, Dr. Guillano was a woman. An older woman. And Bella already had her future mapped out with Jackson.

She hurried toward the room that the doctor had come out of but hesitated at the door. Was that 402? Or 404? She stared at each room, confused as to which one she was supposed to get a blanket for. After a moment, she stepped into 404.

A young girl looked up from her bed. She looked to be in her early teens but frowned when she saw Bella. "Are you cold?" Bella asked.

The girl shook her head, her eyes still wide. Bella put on a smile. "Anything I can get you?" she asked.

"The remote?" Her voice was so small as she made her request.

"Sure," Bella said. That couldn't be a hard thing to come by. But try as she might, Bella couldn't locate it. She dug through drawers, checked under the bed, and even looked through her closets. She frowned, turning around.

The girl giggled as she held up her hand. "Oops," she said.

Bella smirked and shook her head. "Guess you found it," Bella replied.

"Guess so!" The girl shrugged. She turned on her TV and leaned back in bed.

"You can holler if you need anything. The call button is right on your bed."

"Thanks," she said.

Bella left her room and nearly bumped into Dr. Guillano. "There you are," she said. "What are you doing in there?"

"Helping, um…" She hesitated, not sure what the girl's name was. "She couldn't find her remote."

Dr. Guillano tilted her head. "Did you get our patient his blanket?" she asked. "Tye?"

Bella cowered, acid rising in her throat. How could she have made yet another mistake? "Um, well, you see, I couldn't remember the room number."

Dr. Guillano shook her head with a frown. "I can see we have a lot of work to do to get you whipped into shape. One, the blanket. And two…You haven't started the IV fluids for Brad."

Bella winced. That was what she needed to do. "I'm sorry, Leona," she started. "I mean, Dr. Guillano." Bella's eyes widened. "It won't happen again."

She turned around and hurried away from her, worried that Dr. Guillano would already have a bad impression of Bella as a nurse. Somehow, though they had just met, Leona's opinion of her mattered. She was just about to reach the supply closet when she remembered the blanket. She turned around to go back to room 402 but saw Tori was already headed into the room, a blanket in hand.

She groaned and turned back around, then headed to the supply closet to get the items she needed for the fluids. She could picture everyone already talking about her behind her back, joking that she would never make a good nurse if she didn't get it together. Her mind went right back to high school—the teasing, the taunting, the practical jokes. Her peers insisting that she was just plain stupid and had no future doing anything of importance.

She swallowed away the tears and the painful memories to focus on what she needed to do. Just one step at a time. *You got this.*

Still, those thoughts kept running through her mind as she worked on getting Brad's IV started. She reviewed the steps in her mind as she wiped down the back of Brad's left hand with an alcohol wipe. "You'll feel a big pinch," she said, but he didn't even wince. Perhaps he was used to the discomfort that a needle brought on. Quickly, she connected the IV tubing, taped down the cannula with a sense of pride, and entered the fluid rate in the IV pump.

"I'll be back in an hour to check up on you," she said, then squeezed his hand and left his room triumphantly. She was back to feeling a sliver of confidence that she could master this job.

Once she left, she spotted Tori at the computer. There was no better time than the present to see what already was being said about her. She cleared her throat, making Tori look up.

"Hey, Bella," she said.

"So, how upset is Dr. Guillano?" Bella asked.

Tori quickly waved her hand. "Don't worry about it. It's your second shift. Everyone has a few mishaps when they first start. It's how you deal with them that will determine how far you go. Just remember that."

Bella tilted her head. "Thanks for getting the blanket."

The nurse's station light lit up, and Tori looked over and shook her head. "I would ask you to get that, but that wouldn't be fair to you."

Bella leaned over and saw that room 404 was lit up. She frowned. "What do you mean?"

"Isabelle likes to call the nursing staff into the room just because she gets lonely. And if I have to look for her remote one more time when she already has it, I can assure you I might just scream." She laughed. "It's what happens when your mother has to work, leaving you here alone."

The alarm sounded again, and Tori put on a smile. "Just put on a happy smile, and away you go." She turned to go, and Bella watched her. She now was glad she knew the tricks that Isabelle liked to pull, and hopefully she wouldn't fall for it next time. She spotted Dr. Guillano headed her way and quickly jumped behind the desk. If she looked like she was just standing around, that would be another mark against her.

"Hey, Bella, listen," Dr. Guillano started, approaching her. "I don't want us getting started on the wrong foot. I didn't transfer hospitals so I could be the hospital bully. That's not who I am or what I'm about. The truth is, I would like to believe that once you get to know me, you'll realize that I'm just a nice woman who's only trying to help."

Bella nodded, and Dr. Guillano's smile faded slightly. "With that being said, I believe to be the best, you have to learn from the best. And I don't want to sound conceited, but I'm one of the best. And I don't support mistakes. We all have to be better every minute, every hour, and every day than we were the day before. So, I'll be sure that you live up to my beliefs. Do you understand?"

"Yes, ma'am," Bella said, feeling like she needed to salute or something.

"Very well." Dr. Guillano turned from Bella. "For the record, just call me Leona."

She then left, never looking back to make sure her point had gotten across, but Bella heard her loud and clear. She needed to step up. If she tried hard enough, maybe she could be half as confident as Dr. Guillano—Leona. She still wasn't exactly sure how to take the doctor, but she was surely going to do her best to live up to whatever her expectations were.

As she watched Leona walk away, an overwhelming mix of

emotions flooded through Bella. Part of her was giddy about the prospect of seeing Leona again, or her possibly becoming Bella's mentor, and the other part was weighed down with self-doubt. Moments of feeling like she had everything handled were brief and always replaced with the nagging thought: What if I'm not good enough? What if I majorly screw up and everything falls apart?

Bella returned to work. She had to prove those thoughts wrong.

CHAPTER THREE

Leona

When Leona first caught a glimpse of the nurse on duty with her, Bella, her thoughts went to how young she looked. She couldn't possibly be any older than twenty-one years old, right? She wasn't like the nurses Leona was used to seeing in the hospital she worked at in New York. But Leona could tell she had determination, despite her faults. She was also alluring. Leona couldn't deny that she had checked out Bella's figure under her scrubs. She had ample curves and a lovely smile, which had made Leona's heart flutter slightly. She was at work, though, and knew feelings like that were inappropriate.

"Four-zero-seven needs some ice." Leona reached out to take Bella's arm as Bella hurried past her. "And her mother needs two extra pillows. It's going to be a long night for her."

"Yes, ma'am," Bella said, her tone soft. She looked up and met Leona's arched eyebrow. "Leona," she corrected.

Leona let go of her arm and watched her as Bella stepped into the room before letting a small smile play across her face. There was a definite hesitation about Bella, like she was waiting for Leona's next slap across the wrist. She didn't want to hold that kind of power over Bella, so she would need to tread carefully so Bella saw her as more of a coworker. Leona sighed and turned, heading to the front desk where Dr. Whalen stood.

"How's your shift going?" he asked.

"For Bella or me?" Leona asked, smirking.

He dropped his gaze to hers, then chuckled. "For both."

"I'm not in Kansas anymore," Leona teased. "Or, I should say, definitely not New York City."

He crossed his arms around the chart he was holding, pulling it to his chest. "Come on now," he started. "Chicago can't be all that different. Maybe we don't have the high-tech mumbo jumbo machines you have in The Big Apple, but we do pretty well. Heck, it's been just over a year since they remodeled this place. You should have seen it back then."

Leona smiled. "Nah, your hospital is fine. I'm only teasing—more or less. It's Bella, though. What's her story? She seems a bit wet behind the ears if you know what I mean. I get the feeling she's been a nurse for about a day."

He laughed, checking his watch, then leaned against the counter. "You aren't far off. She started last night." Leona's jaw dropped, which brought on another round of laughter. "You see, she's part of this program that we run at Capmed, which is only in its second semester. But if you're in a nursing program and you're in your final semester, you can apply for a position here. It's like a nursing assistant program, through which we shape the way these individuals become nurses. Each floor gets two to three individuals that are welcomed

25

into Capmed to take part. If they succeed by the end of the semester, then typically we try to have a position waiting for them."

"Interesting. So she really is brand new to the field. It's kind of like an externship."

"Except they get paid. They do it along with their schoolwork, so life can get challenging. But that one…" He hesitated, and Leona followed where his hand pointed. Bella had just exited the room and pulled her hair from her ponytail. It cascaded down her shoulders, and Leona had an urge to run her fingers through it. She wanted to smooth the tangled strands, tying it back in a sleek up-do. Then her fingers would trail to the exposed nape of Bella's neck. Then her lips…

"Don't you think?" Dr. Whalen asked.

Leona blinked. She had gotten lost in her fantasy—one she wasn't supposed to be having. "I'm sorry. What was that?" She watched Bella set her hair back up into a tighter bun, then went on along her way.

"I see great potential in her." Dr. Whalen repeated.

"You do?" Leona asked, turning to him.

He smirked. "Let me guess; you don't?"

She shrugged. "I do, but there have been a few issues. She seems a bit forgetful. And I would say her youthfulness isn't going to win her nursing points. For example, there's this one patient that practically had her scouring the room, looking for a remote control that the patient had in her hand."

He laughed. "Isabelle. That's one thing about the pediatric floor. You always have to be on your toes. Otherwise, these patients will run you ragged. Tori still falls for the remote trick." He threw up his hands and shrugged. "It happens. But what I've noticed is Bella Strong has heart, which goes a long way in the nursing profession. I can see that she would be a great asset to this team. I wouldn't count her out just yet." He patted Leona's shoulder, then left to tend to a patient. Leona stared after him, musing on his words. She looked down at her clipboard, then headed toward Brad's room.

She knocked on the door and Bella's voice rang out. "Come on in!"

Leona opened the door and entered the room. She didn't recall telling Bella that Brad needed anything. She herself had only stopped to check in on him. Bella looked up as she finished fluffing a pillow behind him.

"Just getting Brad more comfortable. That huge basketball game is on. Isn't that right, Brad?"

Brad's eyes and rosy cheeks were bright as he nodded eagerly. "That's nice," Leona said.

She cast a look over to Bella, hearing Dr. Whalen's voice in her head. He was right. What Bella had going for her was the compassion she could give to patients. That was something you couldn't train for or be taught. Suddenly Leona didn't want to worry quite so much about the mistakes here and there. She just wanted to help Bella. She wasn't used to monitoring a new nurse, but she also remembered her first days. Medical school had been rough, and she had been a bit clumsy when she had first started working with patients. For that reason, she had a lot of empathy for Bella and wanted to see her succeed.

She watched as Bella interacted with Brad. If she wanted to have kids one day, Bella would make a great mother. Leona's heart squeezed as she ached about her own desires for motherhood. She had always wanted a child, but somehow it had never worked out. And now that she was in her forties, that dream was fading more each year.

She smiled at Bella, pushing her own longings aside. Leona

had a feeling she would really love working at Capmed thanks to a certain nurse.

———

Two hours into the shift, Leona and Bella left another room. Leona looked over to Bella as the young nurse released a yawn. Bella's eyes widened as she covered her mouth. "Excuse me. I'm not quite used to the work schedule yet."

"Well, it has only been like twenty-four hours since you started this routine, right?"

Bella arched an eyebrow, which made Leona smile.

"Let's go grab some coffee."

"What about our rounds?" Bella asked.

"It's called a break. I'm sure even Chicago allows breaks."

Bella's cheeks turned a dark shade of red as they got into the elevator and took it down to the cafeteria. "So, how'd you know?" Bella asked as the elevator dinged and the doors opened.

"Know what?" Leona replied, leading the way.

She noted that Bella picked up the pace to keep up with her, indicating she didn't want to be left in the dust. That was a good sign, and she admired that.

"That I've only worked here twenty-four hours," Bella responded. "Is my work ethic that obvious?"

Leona smirked, turning to face her. "Well, there are obvious things that you need to learn, but that comes with time. No one becomes Florence Nightingale overnight." Leona snickered. "You probably don't even know who that is. You're a young'un."

Bella laughed. "I don't live under a rock. I am in nursing school, after all."

They turned and entered the cafeteria, and Leona continued. " I like to learn who I'm going to be working with because it helps me know what I need to do as the practitioner for my nurse and what my nurse will be able to handle."

She stopped at the coffee cart and put two fingers up for the guy manning the cart, then glanced over at Bella. "Make sense? I'm not simply wanting to be nosy or anything. I just feel it's my due diligence to make sure I know what I'm getting into, as far as a working relationship goes."

Bella nodded. "Can't see anything wrong with that. But may I ask what you've figured out so far? I mean, I know we didn't get off to the best start with me, um…Well, you know." Bella's eyes dropped as Leona paid for the coffees.

"Again, you'll improve as the days, weeks, months, and years go on. That much is clear. I would say there's definite work to be done, but in due time, if you stick with me, you'll be ready to run this place." She handed Bella her coffee.

"You didn't need to pay for my coffee. I can manage." Bella reached in her pants pocket and pulled out a few dollars.

"Keep your money." Leona turned from her and led her way to a corner table. "Everyone makes a few mistakes at the beginning. If I had known you were fresh into this job, I would have expected those mistakes. Going forward, it's what you do to learn from your mistakes. You can always work to be better. That's the goal, and that's what I intend on helping you with."

Bella nodded. They sat in silence for a few minutes as they both sipped on their coffees. Bella's cheeks were flushed and she kept averting her gaze, which gave Leona an opening to really take her in. She watched Bella's full lips perch on the edge of her cup, taking small, timid sips, and she lingered in the dark hues of Bella's eyes as they darted around the room. If she was really going to be working with Bella more and helping her find her place at Capmed, she needed to get this attraction in check.

After a moment, Bella finally met her gaze.

"May I ask a question?"

Leona arched an eyebrow. "On one condition." She scrunched up her lips into a small pucker. "Make that two conditions."

"Which are?"

"One, if I don't like the question, I don't answer it."

"I suppose that's acceptable. What's the second condition?"

"If I agree to answer the question, then you have to answer a question of mine." Leona grinned. "And you can't decline to answer it."

"That hardly seems fair," Bella replied, scrunching up her nose, which elicited a soft chortle from Leona.

"Those are my conditions. So, do we have a deal?"

"Fine. Deal." Leona nodded and motioned with her hand for Bella to proceed. "Why move to Chicago, when you were based in New York City?"

"Now who's checking up on who?" Leona softly replied.

Bella shrugged. "Tori happened to mention it. That's beside the point, though. What brought you here from New York?"

Leona looked down at her pool of black coffee, then lifted it to her lips and sipped. They had known each other only a short time, and she wasn't ready to dive down that rabbit hole with anyone, but she could answer the question without giving Bella a comprehensive picture.

"Have you ever just felt like you needed a change?" Leona asked. Bella gave her a blank look, which made Leona drop her gaze. "Probably not, because you're still a child."

"I'm not a child," Bella argued. "I'm twenty-two years old. That legally qualifies me as an adult, by anyone's standards."

Leona saw she struck a nerve, but she didn't feel the need to apologize. "I'm forty-five," Leona said quietly. "So, by my standards, anyone under thirty is a child."

She paused. "I'm sorry. I won't call you a child again. But... Have you ever felt you needed a change?"

Bella nodded, then hesitated. "I guess maybe I haven't quite gotten there, but I think I know what you mean."

"Then, yeah, I was just at that point. So here I am." She rubbed her hands together. "And on that note..."

Bella's eyes widened. "I think it's time to go back to work now, isn't it?"

Leona chuckled. She would give Bella a reprieve, but when the opportunity arose, once they had gotten to know each other a little bit, she would make sure ask all the questions she wanted the answers to. For now, Leona was just looking forward to spending more time with her.

CHAPTER FOUR

Bella

Bella's phone rang as soon as she stepped foot into the hospital. She gave a weak smile when she saw Jackson's name on the caller ID, requesting a video chat. It was bittersweet for her. While she was glad to get the chance to speak with him, it'd been two weeks since they had last seen each other, and she worried that he would soon get tired of this. What shocked her the most, though, was that she'd barely thought of him during that time. He was the one always calling and texting to try to get them to spend time together. She was...indifferent. Or simply too frazzled from school and work.

His call reminded her that she had yet another thing to juggle: her relationship. Now that she was headed into another shift, she would only be able to spare two minutes. Not nearly long enough to sustain a healthy connection with Jackson.

"Hey," she said, stepping into the elevator.

Wrong move. Immediately his face flickered on the screen, and then he froze. Bella groaned and she quickly punched the button for her floor. "Give me a minute. I'll get off the elevator soon and—"

Her call dropped, and she groaned, falling back against the wall of the elevator. When the doors opened, she stepped off onto her floor and dialed Jackson's number.

"Hello?"

"Sorry, I got in the elevator and lost connection."

"So, you can't do dinner tonight," he said. Just hearing the pain in his voice tore at her chest a little bit. "You're at work."

"I'm sorry," she said. She felt like she had said sorry so many times over the last two weeks. But with her demanding school and work schedules, all free time was devoted to her coursework and sleep. Things had been busy from the beginning, but these past two weeks had her running in circles at twice the speed. "Are you still there?" Bella asked, as Jackson hadn't responded to her apology.

"I'm still here. I'm sorry. I just miss you. That's all."

A weight shifted in her chest. "I know." More guilt ate at her because she realized she didn't feel the same. She did miss hanging out, but not as much as he seemed to miss her. She looked over to the desk where Leona stood, her face immediately warming. It was like she ran a fever every time Leona was around. What was wrong with her body?

She sighed. Another minute standing there, and she'd be late to her shift. She couldn't stand there and chat on the phone, especially when she knew others were looking in. She didn't want to give anyone a reason to think she wasn't doing her job. "I'm sorry, but I have to get going."

"It's all right, I understand," Jackson said flatly. "Have a good day at work."

"I will."

"Love you," he said.

She disconnected the call and hurried over to where Leona stood, who arched an eyebrow and looked up and down at Bella. Bella looked down to see her purse still hanging around her. In a rush to answer Jackson's call, she had come to the floor without dropping her things off in her locker.

"I'm sorry," she mumbled. "I was in such a rush that I didn't stop at the breakroom."

"That call must've distracted you. Was it your boyfriend or something?" Leona asked, turning from Bella.

For some reason, Bella couldn't say yes. She didn't want to talk about Jackson with Leona. "Uh, I'll hurry to the locker and be right back."

"Don't bother," Leona replied, opening up a drawer. "You can lock it up in here."

Bella didn't object as she locked the drawer and turned back to Leona. "Ready for duty," she said, like she was a soldier standing at attention.

Leona nodded, tilting her head slightly. "We have a full day," she said. "For starters, room four-zero-four needs a breathing treatment. Room four-zero-seven needs to be taken down for an X-ray. Room four-zero-two…" She stopped and looked at Bella. "Don't you think you need to take notes?"

"Oh. Right," Bella said, hurrying around the desk to grab a notebook and pen.

Bella jotted down what Leona had told her, ready to add this to the stack of notes she had at home. Despite reviewing her notes before passing out each night, Bella didn't feel like she had gotten that much better at this job. She needed to remind herself that she wasn't an incompetent woman destined to make a mistake at every turn.

There was also the fact that even after three weeks, Leona flustered her. It was most likely because Leona held a seniority position, and it worried Bella that she would mess up in front of Leona and screw up her chances for getting a job at Capmed after her program ended. That, and the sensations Leona stirred in her body.

They got to work, with Bella running around like she did most nights, with very little time to complain about her feet being tired or worry about time creeping to a crawl. That was one definite thing she could say about working at Capmed. There was little time to focus on the day dragging by. That was the best part about the job.

It was when she sunk in a chair to relax during a break that she realized how tired she truly was. She grabbed her water after opening a bottle of aspirin, then downed two pills and sighed. In thirty minutes, the pills would kick in, and she would have some more energy. She stifled a yawn, shaking her hazy head. At least, she hoped so. She tore into her granola bar and flipped open her economics workbook.

"It's not a lifestyle everyone can handle."

Bella looked up when she heard Leona's voice. She gave a weak smile and shrugged. "I'm working on it. Doing what I can to accomplish all my dreams. Isn't that what life is all about?"

Leona quirked up an eyebrow, then let it fall. "I would say so. I should leave you to it."

She turned, and Bella watched her elegant strides. She paused to look over her shoulder, turning her beautiful eyes to Bella. "When you're off your final break, we have an evaluation to get to."

A jolt shot through Bella's spine. "Evaluation?" She stopped mid-chew, gawking at Leona.

"Nothing major. Just something that needs to be done every few weeks. I checked the calendar, and they have me down as your evaluator." She smirked. "I guess it's because I've been the one working with you these last few weeks. This is new to both of us. It shouldn't be too bad, and I'm confident you'll get through it. Enjoy the rest of your break."

With that, she left the breakroom, but the damage had been done. Now she had to focus on what it was that Leona would want to talk to her about. Or how Leona felt about her work habits.

What did Leona really think of her? Probably that she was the clumsiest, most forgetful nurse she'd ever seen and would fail horribly in the end.

Bella closed her eyes and took a breath. It wasn't even about succeeding to prove it to herself and all her old bullies anymore. She wanted to make Leona proud. She felt warm and giddy when Leona smiled at something she'd done well. She wanted more of that smile.

She closed her workbook and stared blankly down at the title. The past three weeks had been a blur. She knew she wasn't being a good girlfriend and she wasn't excelling at work. He grades were also iffy. Though her anxiety often got the best of her, and she knew sometimes her fears were only in her thoughts, what if she really did end up failing? What if she was headed for *the* most epic fail of her life, losing Jackson, her job, and her degree all at once? Her life plan would be ruined.

She needed to stop getting so lost in her worries. Evaluations and tests always did this to her. If she thought too much about something, she would become overanxious.

Fifteen minutes later, she was headed back to work and in search of Leona. Instead, she found Jacqueline, a fellow nursing assistant in the same program as Bella. She stood at the desk, staring at the computer, and when she looked up, she heaved a sigh.

"Bella, you have no idea how glad I am to see you," she said. "The computer froze, and I've tried everything."

"You tried rebooted it?" Bella asked.

Jacqueline nodded. "Even that. But nothing." She slammed her hand down on the desk, frustration etched on her face. "Dr. Whalen asked me to print this patient's chart, and he's already been waiting ten minutes. I'm going to fail this task for sure." Her voice was filled with a despair that Bella had felt so many times.

"You'll be fine. Let me look."

Bella hurried around the desk to inspect the computer as Jacqueline scooted back to make room for Bella. Bella pressed a few keys, then tried the Esc. key, and suddenly, the mouse zipped across the computer. Bella held up her hands and looked over to Jacqueline.

"Not stuck anymore."

"You're a lifesaver," Jacqueline responded, moving up to take a look. "What'd you do?"

"Hit a bunch of keys and said a little prayer," Bella replied with a snort. "Who knows? As long as it's working again."

"Truth," Jacqueline said. The printer whirred to life, and she looked over to Bella. "I'll just get this printed, and Dr. Whalen will be a happy camper."

"So, have you had your evaluation by any chance?" Bella asked.

Jacqueline looked at Bella in horror. "Evaluation? Are you serious? I feel like I'm messing up every thirty seconds, and now I need to be evaluated over that? This can't be for real. How'd you hear about that? *What* did you hear?"

"Don't stress!" Bella quickly retorted. "I'm sure it's no big deal. Leona, I mean, Dr. Guillano just told me that she needed to see me after break to have my review. Something about how we need an evaluation every few weeks. Guess they want to see if you're on track to completing the Capmed program. Who knows?"

She stifled a yawn, then shook her head. "You started a week after me, so yours is probably coming up. But, I have a question…"

Bella's words fell off as she waited for Jacqueline to look at her. Jacqueline nodded at her, and Bella asked, "Are you finding it difficult to have a social life while doing this and going to school?"

Jacqueline laughed. "What social life? I didn't have one before all this landed in my lap. So, to answer your question…" She grabbed the papers from the printer. "Haven't noticed a difference. I'd better get these to Dr. Whalen."

She hurried away from the desk, and Bella thought about what Jacqueline had said. If she didn't have Jackson, then she probably could have said the same, but having a boyfriend really complicated things. *Future husband,* she reminded herself. Jackson would be the father of her kids someday, which made him even more important.

Bella looked toward Leona's office and groaned. She was already ten minutes over her break. She just hoped she didn't get lectured about tardiness. When she reached Leona's office, she lightly tapped on the door. Leona kept her head down at a chart she was reading. "A few minutes later than I expected," she said in greeting.

"I'm sorry. I, uh, you see," Bella stammered. Leona looked up, gawking at her as she responded like an idiot. "Jacqueline had computer issues, and I was helping her out."

"I see," Leona said. "Close the door behind you."

That was never a good sign. Was she about to be yelled at for her inability to handle the job? She thought she was doing well enough, but if that were the case, why did the door need to be closed?

She probably just doesn't think everyone should hear what stellar work you're doing. It might make people jealous. That was one way to look at it. It sure sounded much better than the alternative.

As Bella sat down, she crossed her legs, then uncrossed them. She fidgeted in her seat, then sat up straight. Her body felt restless as she stared straight ahead, just hoping that the whole thing wouldn't be a bust.

"No need to be nervous," Leona said.

"You can tell?" Bella said, releasing a nervous giggle.

"The fidgeting gave it away." Leona smiled, leaning across the desk to grab a notebook. "As mentioned, I'm not even sure what to expect out of this. So, we're just going to wing it together. Sound like a plan?"

"Oh, yeah, sure." Bella stared.

How was Leona always so confident and easygoing about everything? It was a trait that never failed to draw Bella toward her. If relaxed is what Leona wanted her to be, then that was what she was going to be. But even the easy tone of Leona's voice didn't do anything to soften Bella's worry. Hopefully, that would work itself out once the evaluation began.

"I'm going to ask you a few questions, and then we'll sort of go into any thoughts, worries, or brutal beatings."

"What?" Bella squealed.

Leona snickered. "Kidding. Just relax. I'm not here to belittle you as an employee or as a person. There's nothing I can say that can cause you harm if you don't let it. Got that?"

Bella thought about it. No, she wasn't sure she quite understood it, but she simply nodded.

"Great. Shall we begin? For starters, tell me about Bella Strong."

Bella's eyes wandered nervously around the room. That seemed like an offhanded question, not to mention extremely vague. What was the point of Leona asking that? How was it related to her evaluation?

She hesitated for what felt like ages, her face warm from the beating lights that shot down on her. Was she sweating? She felt like she was sweating. Again, she started to fidget, but that was because Leona had a way of looking at Bella and making her feel like Leona was boring holes into Bella's mind.

Bella cleared her throat. "Tell you about me? Like, what are you looking for?"

Leona leaned back in her chair, clasping her hands together. "Shall I rephrase the question?"

"That might be best," Bella mumbled.

"All right. What made you want to become a nurse? Your influences, your ambitions, your passions, etcetera. Does that help?"

"Somewhat," Bella whispered. "Well, I guess I would start with my mom. She's a nurse. Or was, I mean."

"She got out of it?" Leona asked.

"It's not that she got out of it, exactly. She loved being a nurse, or so I was told. She decided to start a family and thought nursing would take away from her passion of being a mom. But she's told me stories about helping people, and that intrigued me to give it a shot."

"How many siblings do you have?"

"There are three of us. My older brother, who's just about to turn thirty, then me, then my younger sister, who's fourteen."

"Gosh, seems like the family tree spans over several years as far as the kids' branches go." Leona arched an eyebrow. "I would guess there's a story there as to why she waited so long between your brother and you and then again from you to your sister." Her eyes darted away. "Not that you need to share that story if you don't want to."

"I don't mind. As I've heard it, my parents wanted to spend

time with each of their children before bringing another one into the mix. They wanted to make sure all of us felt loved. They might have had another after Veronica was born, but an accident changed that."

Bella stopped speaking after that and looked down at her hands, which were clasped tightly together. She unlatched them and looked back up; Leona's gaze had drifted at the same time Bella's had.

Leona cleared her throat and nodded. "I see." She looked down at the notebook in front of her, then back up to Bella. "So, it looks like you had a fine upbringing that led you to help people. That makes sense."

"It does? How so?"

"Well, when I see you interact with the patients, it's like you're speaking to their soul. That's one thing you excel in, and I can assure you that it's a quality that doesn't go unnoticed."

Bella felt her cheeks getting warm. That was nice to hear. Now, if only they could say the same about her nursing abilities. She knew she had a ways to go before she could be called a stellar nurse. After all, she was still learning so much. But she was always willing to adapt, and she hoped that would account for something.

"I do have concerns, but they are limited, " Leona continued. Bella grabbed onto her chair, bracing herself for what Leona was about to thrust upon her. "I saw the way you were with the foster kids that were here a few weeks ago, but there are only so many places empathy can take you. You also need strong skills to succeed in a hospital. I'm not trying to sound cruel but...Are you sure nursing is the right profession for you?"

Bella faltered. She had always wanted to follow in her mother's footsteps, no matter how hard it was. Maybe Leona was simply trying to build her resolve.

"Well, those kids didn't have anyone," Bella began. "So I

wanted to spend more time assisting them. I'm sorry if I spent too much time with them."

Leona waited for Bella to answer her question. When she didn't, Leona repeated, "Are you sure nursing is for you? Some people just aren't cut out for nursing, and that's entirely okay."

"So, you don't think this is something I'm capable of?"

"I didn't say that," Leona started. "Everyone is capable of everything if they put their mind to it. But does that necessarily mean you should strive for that? Why not put yourself in a place that you would shine?"

Bella looked down at her fists. "I want to be a nurse," she stated firmly. "I can be a nurse. All I've wanted is to follow in my mom's footsteps and help people." She stopped short of going into a rant about how much her bullies had hurt her and how she just wanted to do her part to take away other people's pain.

Leona sat back in her chair and smiled. "Good. Remember that. On days when you feel you've made a lot of mistakes, remember your reason for being here. Prove to me that you really want this. Otherwise, you should consider a new career path."

Bella looked up, surprised. She felt inspired and crushed at the same time. Could she prove she belonged here? She hoped she could. Changing careers wasn't in her plan.

———

Two days had passed, and Bella still couldn't get what Leona had said out of her mind. Was she fighting a losing battle and attempting to do nursing only because it was her mother's passion? She did want to help people, but there were other careers through which she could do that. The way the evaluation had ended had left Bella determined but a bit shaken. While Leona had said that there wasn't one major issue with Bella's work habits, she *had* said that Bella needed to reconsider her drive. Bella didn't want to back down from her goals, especially when that would mean revising her whole life plan. And trying to pivot now would be admitting defeat, that she wasn't good enough to be a nurse.

"You look like you have a world of thoughts lying on your shoulders."

She looked up to see Tori at the desk, her eyes homed in on Bella. Bella had been staring at the computer screen and aimlessly tapping her pencil in time to her thoughts. She dropped her pencil and let out a little laugh.

"You've got that right." She covered her face and shook her head, hoping that she wouldn't burst into tears right there in front of Tori. That was something she definitely wanted to avoid. "Can I talk to you about something? Maybe a few things?"

"Sure. I have time. Want to go in my office?"

Bella looked around the empty corridors and shook her head. "Here's fine. First of all, why did I get put on Dr. Guillano's rotation instead of Dr. Whalen's? I thought that we worked well together, Dr. Whalen and I. I know it was only one shift, but even you said he said I had potential, right? So, why the change? Jacqueline could have easily been placed with Dr. Guillano when she started. I just don't get it."

Tori frowned. "Is something wrong? Are you and Dr. Guillano not meshing well together? I thought it would be something that would work, especially since she asked for you to be on her rotation."

"She asked for me?" Bella asked, her jaw dropping.

Tori nodded. "You were only supposed to be with her for one night. Dr. Whalen was off the rest of the week, so when Jacqueline started, it was intended that you would switch back to Dr. Whalen because he thought it was a good fit. However, Dr. Guillano insisted, and Dr. Whalen, being as chill as he is, didn't object. He even thought that maybe you would be better off with her because she came from New York and could teach you some of the finer things. He thought it would be a good move for you, and we didn't think anything of it. It was a mutual decision, and it was an easy transition to keep you with Dr. Guillano and put Jacqueline with Dr. Whalen. But if you feel that it isn't the right fit, then maybe we need to do some adjusting."

"It's not that," Bella quickly commented. She leaned against her chair. In reality, she thought that maybe Leona would have been better off without her. She was still making a lot of mistakes and probably causing Leona a lot of headaches. Was Leona just feeling sorry for her? That thought made her queasy. She didn't want her pity.

"I just had no idea. I thought it was something you decided based on the schedules. But if she asked for me, then maybe I'm mistaken."

"Something has clearly happened, though. Wanna talk about it?" Tori leaned against the desk, her eyes locked on Bella's.

Now, Bella wondered if maybe she was opening up a can of worms that she wasn't prepared for. It was best to leave it unsaid, right? But keeping her thoughts and emotions bottled up inside could derail her progress in her training, and her training meant everything for her.

Bella took a deep breath, steeling herself for what she was about to say.

"The other day, I was in Dr. Guillano's office to go over my evaluation." Tori raised an eyebrow, but didn't interrupt, so Bella continued. "Ultimately, she had nothing negative to say, but some of her comments got me thinking…like if nursing is right for me. I'm starting to doubt my choices. I want to help people, but I've focused on being a nurse mostly because that's what my mom did. And it fits well in my life. Plus, I've put four years on hold to be a nurse. But what if I'm just not suited for this and everything I've worked toward is a waste? Because I..."

Bella stopped short of saying she was a failure. She had achieved a lot over the years, but somehow her self-doubts always crept back in. And being so clumsy at nursing so far wasn't helping.

"But why would Dr. Guillano make this suggestion?" Tori asked. "She must've felt she had a reason to say something."

Bella sighed. "I don't know. She said that I show a lot of empathy with the patients. Like when the foster kids were here from Indiana." She shrugged. "I love children, and I don't see why that can't mean I would make a great pediatric nurse. I was left a little confused, like she was hinting that nursing isn't for me."

Tori scrunched up her face. "Looks to me like maybe you didn't take the time to try to get some real answers from her. Ultimately, though, I would say she's only trying to help. All communication I've had with Dr. Guillano has been positive. I really wouldn't worry too much about the matter. But if you want answers, sometimes you just have to insist on them."

Tori looked at Bella oddly before continuing. "But I'm also a little confused about one thing. Did you say your evaluation? What evaluation?"

"The one that we have to go through every few weeks." Bella shrugged. "I don't know, she said it's to make sure we're on the correct path or something."

Tori tilted her head. "I know nothing of that. Guess I'll be looking into that myself. The only evaluation I know of is the end-of-the-program evaluation. That's when they'll either recommend you for a position or see about placing you elsewhere."

Tori's phone started ringing, and she looked down at it. "I have to take this, but I would say you should talk to her. Couldn't hurt." She then answered the call and turned away from the desk.

Bella got up from the nurse's station and headed straight for Leona's office. She had plenty to discuss with her—for starters, why she felt the need to lie to her about the evaluation. Something was wrong, and she wasn't leaving her office until she had all the answers, whether good or bad.

CHAPTER FIVE

Leona

A knock sounded on her door. Leona looked up from her work and saw Bella, whose eyes seemed to have darkened instantly. Leona felt there was a strong sense of urgency as to why Bella was there.

"Bella!" she exclaimed. "Do you need something? I thought I'd just head downstairs to the cafeteria for lunch. Wanna join me?" Leona stood up from her desk, but Bella remained standing by the door, her expression stony.

"I need to get this out there," Bella said, taking two steps into her office. "Why did you want me on your rotation and what was that fake evaluation all about? I talked to Tori, and she knows nothing of an evaluation save for the end-of-program one."

Leona dropped her gaze to her desk. Well, this wasn't exactly something she thought she would have to rush right out to explain. But it was out there, and she couldn't back down from it. If Bella needed answers, then she would give those answers.

"How about you let me get you lunch, and I'll explain?" Leona moved around her desk. "It's my treat, so what do you have to lose? An hour of your time having a meal with me?" She laughed. "And I'll give you the answers you need."

Bella looked over her shoulder, like she was looking for someone. Leona stepped in closer to her and Bella finally turned back around and nodded. "Fine, but I hope this isn't a trap."

Leona moved past her and out her door. She was going to have some serious explaining to do, and she just hoped that Bella wouldn't be upset once she spilled everything out to her. She didn't think she was being mischievous in her attempt to have Bella assigned to her.

She supposed, looking back, it might seem like she had been deceptive, but her intentions were good, if not a bit misguided. Bella had intrigued her, from her looks all the way to her compassion for her patients. She had a yearning to get to know Bella, an interest she tried not to think about too much since it was beyond work appropriate. But she liked to think she could separate her personal and professional life. Above everything, she wanted to mentor Bella and help her gain more confidence so she could succeed. Plus, she had just ended a relationship three months ago and wasn't eager to jump into another one.

They each got their food and headed to a table, where Bella seemed quiet and reserved. She had barely spoken two words when they were ordering their lunch.

"You're not very talkative," Leona began.

"Just processing, I suppose," Bella quietly remarked. "Not sure what you're going to tell me in order to explain the secrecy and all, but I guess I'll soon find out. Right?"

"That's the plan," Leona replied, taking a bite of her salad. She slowly chewed on her food, then swallowed it. Bella didn't strike her as someone who would wait too long to get the answers she wanted. It wasn't like she could wait for Bella to forget about it.

"So, what'd you ask?" Leona joked. Bella looked up, making Leona laugh. "I'm kidding. You want to know why I wanted you on my rotation?"

"Or, rather, why you didn't tell me that you purposely asked for me," Bella responded. "That would be a nice start."

Leona shrugged. "I guess I didn't think it was that big of a deal. When I first started here, I felt like it was a huge change. I was coming into new surroundings, and I guess a part of me didn't want to be the new one in town. You know? When I heard good things from Mitch…Dr. Whalen, it seemed to click that maybe you were the one I should have working rounds with me. It was out of respect that I felt compelled to pull you on my rotation. I didn't tell you because I didn't think it was something I had to say. Plus, I thought that maybe you wouldn't want to work with me every shift. I didn't want you to think I was forcing you to do something you didn't want to do."

"I suppose I can understand that," Bella responded.

Leona exhaled, happy that explanation was enough. Was she doing the wrong thing, putting herself in closer proximity to a nurse she had romantic interest in? No, she was only trying to help Bella. She could ignore the attraction. And Bella might be in a relationship, which made everything complicated. Bella seemed stressed, and revealing her interest in her young mentee would only stress her out more. They were coworkers and that's how it would stay.

"Happy to hear," Leona said, digging into her salad and ignoring the fact that Bella's eyes were still on hers. As the minutes dragged on, she couldn't ignore it any further. "Oh, yeah," she mumbled. "You had another question."

Bella nodded. "Tori knew nothing about said evaluation. She's the head nurse, and I would think that she would know what evaluations needed doing. So, I'm guessing that was only a ruse. What I don't know is, why?"

Leona dropped her fork and took a long swig of her water. "I believe, in the beginning, I told you that I like to get to know the people I work with. A few weeks ago, we were talking, and you seemed to not want to give any answers or be open personally. This was my way of getting to know you a little bit more." She sighed, taking another drink. "I'm sorry for making it happen in a not-so-normal manner. I shouldn't have lied to you. For that, I sincerely apologize."

Bella shook her head, staring down at her fries and sandwich. It looked like she was processing the news and not sure how to take it. "I don't want the fact that I falsely said you were being evaluated to cloud our working relationship, Bella. I really am sorry."

Bella sighed. "What I don't get," she began, looking up for the first time since Leona apologized, "is how you don't think I'm cut out to be a nurse. That upset me."

"I did not say that," Leona argued. "I wanted to know your reasons for being a nurse and help you be open to the possibility that there are other careers out there. There's a learning curve here, but it's also okay to consider a different option if things don't work out. I only said that because you always seem so stressed, and nursing should be your passion. And again, that's not a negative thing. That's all."

Bella looked like she was going to say something, but Leona held up her hand. "Let me finish, please. I think you're a hard worker and that you've grown as an employee over the past few weeks. That's saying a lot. I worked with a lot of people in New York, and I would definitely say they would be better off not working in a hospital. You told me why you decided to become a nurse, and I admire your reasons. I absolutely think you could make a fine nurse. Don't believe that I'm saying you're not capable, because I don't feel that way—only that you should remain open to new possibilities. I would give that advice to anyone."

She paused when she saw Bella's eyes softening quite a bit. "If I hurt your feelings in any way, I'm sorry." She wanted to reach out to touch Bella's hand but stopped herself. That wouldn't be a very coworker-like gesture.

"Thank you," Bella replied.

In that moment, relief washed over Leona; Bella even held a slight smile on her lips. Maybe they could get into their meal and just relax and enjoy it. Bella's phone buzzed, and she checked the screen, rolling her eyes.

Leona couldn't resist probing because she didn't get a definite answer last time she fished for information about Bella's personal life. "Boyfriend trouble?" she asked casually.

Bella gave a slight nod, focusing on her food again.

Though Leona's stomach sank, she was glad Bella was in a relationship. It might help Leona keep her distance.

Before she could think of how to change the subject, her phone vibrated and she checked the message, frowning.

Trauma alert in the ER department. Young male bicyclist, hit by a car. Patient, Bradly Carver.

Leona looked up, her eyes wide.

"Something wrong?" Bella asked.

Leona hesitated, then nodded. "It's fine, though. Finish up your meal and I'll see you back at work in fifteen. I have to take care of this."

"Is it a patient? I can come back early and clock in." Bella stood up, but Leona needed first to see what she was coming into. If this was the Brad Carver they had seen a few weeks ago, she didn't want Bella to walk headfirst into the scene without knowing what they were up against.

"It's all right. You enjoy the rest of your food. No need for you to come." Leona got up and grabbed her salad. "See you upstairs."

She hurried and dropped the food into a garbage bin and briskly walked out of the cafeteria and to the elevator, hoping that Bella wouldn't see the urgency in her movement.

She took the elevator up to the main floor to the ER and didn't stop until she reached the front desk. "Where is he?" she asked.

"Trauma room three," the woman behind the desk said. "The trauma team is evaluating him, but I saw on the chart that he was in your service the last time he was here. I thought you should know."

"Thanks." She quickly moved away from the desk and headed to the room.

When she entered, a man was looking down at Brad, speaking firmly but kindly. "You're going to be okay, buddy." A surgeon in scrubs was examining the boy while a nurse stood at his side, assessing the wounds on his body.

"My name is Dr. Leona Guillano. I took care of Brad last time he was here. Can you tell me what happened and what relation you are to the patient?"

The man turned to her, his eyes glossy. "My name is Shane. I, I'm..." He turned back to look at Brad. "I'm the one that hit him." He shook his head. "I don't know what happened. It was all a blur."

"Everything's going to be all right," Leona responded. "Just please wait outside."

As Leona turned to Brad, the trauma surgeon began barking out orders for X-rays and blood work. Leona's heart started racing. She'd help the trauma team get the situation under control and then let Bella know what was going on. There would be plenty of time to ask questions later.

———

Leona grabbed the phone, then dropped it back into the cradle. How was she going to start the conversation? *Hello, Bella? Brad was brought to the emergency room and just transferred to the ICU.*

It still felt so unreal. How could a young child like that be playing one minute and the next, fighting for his life? If anything, that only showed how fragile life was. There wasn't a minute to waste in telling Bella the news.

She grabbed the phone again and dialed upstairs to the pediatric ward. She was surprised Bella hadn't already gotten the news, but if she had, Leona was confident Bella would have rushed downstairs to see Brad for herself. Bella had compassion like that.

"This is Tori," a voice answered.

"Hey, Tori. It's Dr. Guillano. Is Bella around?"

"Ummmmm…Oh yes, there she is. I'll grab her for you. Bella, it's Dr. Guillano."

Leona tapped her fingers on the desk and stared down at the counter. When she noticed her tapping, she quickly stopped and slipped her hand into her pocket to get rid of her nerves.

"Hello?"

"Hey, Bella. I need you to come down to the ER for a minute."

"Is everything okay? Are they short-staffed? What's going on?" Bella rattled off at least a dozen more questions in the time it took for Leona to release a breath.

"I'll discuss it with you once you get down here. Please."

"I'll be right there," Bella said, just before Leona dropped the phone back into the cradle.

While she waited for Bella to arrive, Leona recalled how she had quickly left the cafeteria to get to the ER when she got the text about Brad, but things had seemed to be improving slowly over their conversation. That was a relief, because it meant that hope wasn't all lost for them to find a good working relationship.

It wasn't long before the elevator doors opened and Bella stepped out of the small enclosure. She headed over to where Leona stood, and Leona quickly grabbed her arm and escorted her away from the main lobby.

"Now you're scaring me," Bella mumbled.

"Sorry, I just need to do this away from everyone," Leona said, pulling her into a small and secluded office. After she closed the door, she turned to Bella's wide-eyed expression. "Do you remember Brad Carver?" Leona asked.

"Yeah. The little boy from the foster home in Indianapolis. How could I forget?" Bella's eyes bugged out. "Is he sick? Is he here?"

She started to push past Leona, but Leona reached out and touched her arm. "Hold on, Bella. He's here, but you can't see him quite yet. He was involved in a vehicle-pedestrian accident. A truck didn't see him and rounded the corner. He rode his bike right into this man's path and he was rushed here, and he's in critical condition."

Bella turned and stared at Leona; tears stuck in the corner of her eyes. "I don't understand. What's he doing in Chicago?"

Leona shrugged. "All I know is that they decided to keep him in Chicago in case he had any more health issues and the Indy foster home was overrun with children. A family fostered him immediately once he got put into the system. Unfortunately, this family has six kids already, many of whom are fighting health issues, and they weren't observant enough when he went out on his bike."

"Where is he?" Bella asked.

"He was just moved to the ICU. He'll have some of the best doctors supervising him, but both of his legs are broken, and he has broken ribs. He also has a head contusion. It's a bumpy ride for him, but they're all confident that they'll be able to nurse him back to health."

"And his foster parents?" Bella asked.

"They're here and being questioned, as is the guy that hit him. He didn't run, so that's a good thing. If he hadn't gotten him to the hospital in record time, we could have had a much worse situation."

"I want to see him," Bella replied quietly.

Leona nodded. She knew that Bella would want to have a chance to visit him, but Leona had to prepare her first. "You aren't used to seeing patients like this. You have to be certain you're prepared for that."

"I want to see him," Bella said again, with no hesitation.

Leona led the way out of the room and headed across the hallway. When they walked into the room, they were the only ones in there. She looked over to Bella and saw that Bella's eyes were red. Leona reached out and touched her arm.

"You have to be strong for him. Understand that?"

Bella nodded.

"I'll give you a few minutes."

Leona left, allowing Bella some time alone. When she got out into the hallway, she looked over to the waiting room, where the couple that currently fostered Brad was sitting. They were talking, and she even saw a few smiles and chuckles shared between the two of them. Those smiles bothered her.

When she approached them, the woman looked up and her face turned solemn. "How he's doing?" she asked.

"Mrs. Chadwick, with all due respect, I question if you really care."

Mrs. Chadwick's eyes bugged out and her jaw dropped. "How dare you?" her husband bristled.

"He's six years old. How could you leave him outside by himself, long enough that he would dart into a street? Anything could have happened, but you were too bothered to even pay attention to the littlest child that needed you."

"You don't know us," Mrs. Chadwick said, standing up from her chair.

Leona didn't flinch. "I know that I saw you two laughing just now. This child might not ever laugh again. If he dies, that's on you, and I know for a fact CPS will revoke your foster license."

"Is that a threat?" Mr. Chadwick asked.

Leona tossed a look over to him and shook her head. "No threat, just saying that if I have my say you won't ever get the chance be the cause of any other child in pain again." With that, she spun on her heel and hurried back to the hallway, just as Bella stepped out of Brad's room. Bella met Leona's eyes.

"How is he?" Leona asked.

"He looks so fragile." She looked past Leona and Leona saw a darkness in Bella's eyes. "Are those his foster parents?" she asked.

Leona nodded and Bella started to walk toward them, but Leona pulled her back.

"I took care of it," she said. "I'm sure they got my message."

Bella shot a look to Leona, and they stood there for a short while, their eyes locked on each other.

Leona slowly pulled her hand away from the place on Bella's lower back. She had felt heat radiating up her spine when she touched her, but she had to force herself to step away from her. "I'm sorry I had to be the one to tell you the news."

Bella slowly nodded. "I'm glad you did, though." She sighed

and looked over to the room. "We should probably get back to work."

"You don't have to stay, you know. If you feel you're not in the mood, I can cover for you. You're free to get out of here."

"If I leave, I'll probably get stuck thinking about Brad the entire time I'm home, so I might as well just stay."

Leona understood that, but she wasn't sure Bella would concentrate as they worked the rest of the shift. But she wasn't going to be the one that pushed her to leave, especially when Leona wanted to keep tabs on her and make sure she wasn't falling into a depressed state. If this was how she could watch out for Bella, she wouldn't complain about that.

CHAPTER SIX

Bella

Bella kept her hand on top of Brad's. The longer she stayed there, the smaller he seemed to get. It'd been three days, and he still hadn't opened his eyes. The doctor said it was normal, as his brain was healing, and she shouldn't worry about it, but that was all Bella could do. Worry. She bowed her head.

"Lord, he's too young to come to you. Please watch over this little guy."

She opened her eyes and stared at Brad's little face. The swelling had gone down, so that was a good sign. Another thing the doctors had told her. She brushed her hand across his cheek. She just wanted to see him open his eyes. She looked down at her watch and groaned. If she didn't leave, she would be late for her class.

"I'll see you tomorrow, Brad," she whispered. "Rest well." She squeezed his hand, then got up from the bed. She turned just in time to see Leona turning to leave. Bella cleared her throat, making

Leona turn to look at her. "I didn't hear you come in," Bella said. Leona kept the door open and Bella stepped through, Leona following after her.

"Didn't mean to interrupt. I thought you left work an hour ago, though."

"I didn't have to be at school quite yet and thought I would check up on our patient. Well, not our patient, but you know what I mean…" Bella's voice dropped, and Leona simply nodded. "That doesn't change the fact that you were about to leave, like you didn't want me to know you were there."

Leona gave a weak smile. "It wasn't that I didn't want you to know I was there. I just wanted to give you ample time to spend time with him. Any change?"

"In three days, there hasn't been a single change. But Dr. Boxell said that's not necessarily a bad thing. No change also means he isn't getting worse. So that's promising."

"Right," Leona replied, her eyes a tinge brighter. "Gotta look at the positives."

Bella nodded. "Are you still working?" Bella asked. "It was nice of you to check up on him."

"Well, I just thought that I would check to make sure his health wasn't getting worse. Didn't expect to bump into you." She lifted her gaze to Bella's. "You really should get home, though. You look exhausted."

Bella groaned. She felt exhausted. Every bit of her body ached, and she would have done anything to crawl into bed at that very moment, or at least slip into a nice warm bath. "Class starts in twenty minutes. I don't think I'll be getting rest anytime soon. But that's okay because in the end it will be all worth it, right?" Bella laughed and covered her face in dismay.

"It will be worth it, if you don't work yourself into the ground. That's the fine line you're fighting."

Leona reached out and touched Bella's arm. Bella dropped her hands from her face, making eye contact with Leona. There was an instant spark the moment Leona touched her. Bella tried to steady herself, but the warmth of having Leona near was undeniable. It seemed to grow every shift they spent together, and they even seemed to be growing closer.

But Bella feared that maybe they were getting too close. Leona was a woman, and Bella couldn't be having these kinds of reactions. On the other hand, maybe it was the lack of sleep that was quickly making her mind all weird. Yeah, it was definitely just her being delusional and sleep deprived. Bella was sure.

"I'll do my best to get some rest, but I'm sure I'll be fine," Bella said, quickly stepping away from Leona. "I really should be getting changed and heading to class."

"Of course. I'll see you tomorrow?"

Bella nodded. "I'll be here, bright-eyed and everything." Bella smiled, which seemed to bring a smile to Leona. Bella waved goodbye and turned, heading to the elevator. Once she was inside and the doors were closed, she leaned back against the elevator wall. Leona's smile still played in her mind and part of her didn't want to push that image away.

The doors opened, and she headed to the breakroom, relieved no one was in there. She reached her locker and pulled her clothes out, able to change in private.

She grabbed her purse and bag of scrubs, then slammed her locker shut. The sooner she got out of the hospital, the sooner she would be able to get Leona out of her mind. Or so she hoped. It slowly felt like Leona was the only thing she could think about these days.

As Bella pulled into the parking lot of her school, her phone started ringing. She looked over at the caller ID on her Bluetooth and her face fell—which made her instantly regret that feeling. "Hey," she said, answering the call.

"I've missed you," Jackson said, making her heart tug even harder. That wasn't what she wanted him to say, especially when she had her mind focused on another person. But it was the one thing that made her push Leona out of her head.

"I know. I promise we'll get together soon. Work is even more hectic than before. There's this boy and…Well, we'll hopefully be able to discuss that soon."

Jackson sighed. "It feels so long since we've seen each other. But I know your heart. And while it's a struggle now, it's only short-lived. Before we know it, you'll be graduated and we'll be able to spend all the time we have together. Right?"

Bella fell back against her seat. Jackson was so supportive, and it only made her guilt about not being able to plan dates worse. With everything going on at the hospital, she hadn't even thought of graduation. But it was true. With only three months and two days to go until she graduated, they would have every reason to believe that they would be able to be together every minute after that. Sure, she would hopefully still have a job, but it wouldn't be the mountain of work she was currently experiencing.

Then there would be marriage and children, and everything would fall into place, just the way she had planned. Somehow, that thought didn't give her as much comfort anymore.

"Right?" Jackson asked again.

"Oh. Of course. We'll have the rest of our lives together after just a few more stressful months. Unfortunately, I have to run to class now. Sorry I can't talk longer. I don't want to be late and have everyone stare at me again. That's never fun." She gave a light laugh. "But I hope to see you soon, Jackson. We'll talk later."

"Okay. Love you. Bye."

She hung up and hurriedly jumped out of the car to run

through campus, stepping foot inside her classroom two minutes before her class would begin. It was time to refocus her thoughts on her schoolwork and put both Jackson and Leona to the side.

———

"THERE'S SOMETHING I NEED TO TELL YOU, BELLA."

The way Leona looked at her had Bella clenching her jaw. What was it that Leona wanted to tell her? And where were they? Everything seemed...surreal? But Bella didn't have time to think about that as she moved closer to Leona, feeling the heat from their bodies intertwine. What would it be like to kiss Leona? Would her lips be soft?

Jackson always had dry lips. His kisses were nice, but somehow Bella imagined a kiss from Leona would be on a new level. Electric.

"I'm all ears," Bella gasped.

Leona looked ready to pounce, which sent Bella's mind reeling with fantasies she never let herself admit to. She couldn't be thinking these dirty thoughts about her superior, yet all she wanted was to crash their lips together, give herself completely to this kind, confident, and charismatic older woman. Leona always listened to her and kept her grounded, even when she freaked out about yet another work mistake. Leona gave her confidence, and it was making Bella's urges for her more intense. Maybe it was time to finally give in.

Leona moved closer, whispering, "There's a girl in room four-one-two that needs ice water."

Bella frowned. If Leona kept things this heated, then Bella would also need ice water. But Leona turned away from her, and that only confused Bella even more. Maybe she was reading the signs all wrong. Had she been that crazy to think that Leona would ever be sexually attracted to her?

Bella went to grab the water and ice, which had suddenly appeared on a table that had come out of nowhere. She shook her head, heading to the room with glass in hand. She was there to do a job and needed to remind herself of that as many times as she had to. She wasn't there to fantasize over the doctor, as if she were reading one of those erotic romance novels.

When she got to the room, she saw that it was all…pink. There was no patient, only a big, plush bed. She saw Leona standing in front of her. She was naked from the waist up. Bella's jaw dropped, and she dropped the glass, which shattered.

"What are you doing?" Bella stuttered, though she wasn't opposed to whatever it was that was going on. Leona was sexy and alluring.

Leona had this sensual smirk on her face as she moved closer to Bella. "Do you think it's gone unnoticed the way you look at me? Because I can assure you it hasn't. Those eyes of yours have been locked on me every minute for the last week. And I've loved it."

She grabbed Bella's hand and pulled her closer. With one tug, she placed Bella's hand over her right breast and squeezed. "How does that feel?" Leona whispered.

Bella could only let out a soft moan before Leona passionately pulled her into a kiss. Leona sat down on the bed, pulling Bella down on her. Bella straddled her legs, and they enthusiastically made out with one another inside the hospital room. The front of Bella's pants were already warm and moist from the way Leona passionately kissed her, embracing her and then slowly groping her. Their tongues thrashed wildly against one another. Bella cupped each of Leona's breasts in her palms, kneading them thoroughly between her fingers as Leona made energetic noises of pleasure.

Leona pulled away from the embrace as Bella flicked Leona's nipples between her fingers. Leona's jaw clenched, and she smiled.

"Now what?" Bella panted.

"You should get your phone," Leona said, licking her lower lip.

Bella frowned. Her phone?

She then heard the faint sound of her phone and jerked awake. Bella stared at the books that sat open in front of her, the fog of sleep slow to clear from her mind even as her heart erratically pounded inside her chest.

It was only a dream, even though it had felt so real.

She reached out and grabbed her phone. Jackson's name flashed on the screen. After the heated dream she had just woken up from, the last thing she wanted to do was talk to Jackson. But that was also the reason she had to answer the phone. She felt guilty that it wasn't him featuring in her erotic dreams. Why was she getting so obsessed with another woman?

"Hey," she answered, stifling a yawn. "Good thing you called me because I fell asleep studying and I have a test in a couple of days that I need to focus my attention on."

He laughed. "That's my job," he said.

That brought a slight smile to Bella's lips. "Anyway, good to hear from you."

"Well, thought I would call and see if you had school or work tomorrow evening?"

Bella leaned back in her seat. She had a twelve-hour shift and then expected—or hoped—she would get a full eight hours of sleep before she had classes the following day. But hearing him inquire about her plans left her thinking. Maybe, to get out of her head, she should do what she could to make sure they did get together.

"Were you thinking dinner?" she asked.

"You guessed it. I just think we could use this. What do you say? I won't pester you about it, but I hope it works out."

She couldn't turn down those words. Even though she needed the rest, she had to do something to salvage her relationship with Jackson. "I'm free. Let's do this."

"Great! I'll text you the details after I get a reservation. Can't wait to see you."

"Same." She hung up and nodded to herself. That was the best option to get together with her boyfriend, and then she could stop fantasizing about another person, especially her older female boss.

Bella looked at her anatomy book, which was opened on the kitchen table. She tried focusing on the words on the pages, but the dream invading her mind. She closed the book and sighed. There wasn't any use. If she couldn't get Leona out of her mind, she might as well go to bed and study tomorrow during her breaks. Hopefully, the dream would be out of her system and she wouldn't get caught up in more crazy thoughts by then. At that moment, there wasn't much hope in that.

CHAPTER SEVEN

Leona

"Any pain here?" Leona asked as she pressed on Cassidy Black's stomach. The twelve-year-old winced, and Leona smiled. "Got my answer. I'll have a nurse get the surgeon prepared. We'll get that appendix out tonight."

"Mom!" the girl said, shooting a panicked look past Leona.

Leona chuckled and looked over her shoulder at the concerned expression on Cassidy's mother. "The sooner we get this appendix out, the better. We don't want it to burst. The surgeon on call is one of the best." She winked at Cassidy. "You're going to be just fine."

"Thank you, Dr. Guillano," her mother said, stepping up to her daughter's side.

"My pleasure." She looked back at Cassidy. "I'll leave you alone for a while. Just imagine how much better you'll feel this time tomorrow. Trust me. You'll be thanking me."

Cassidy simply nodded, and Leona left her room. She walked

to the front desk, where Tori sat, on the phone. Tori looked up just as she approached. "Just in time. This call is for you."

Leona grabbed the phone from her. "Will you let the surgeon know we have the surgical consent for Cassidy Black and she's ready to go? The sooner the better."

"Oh, sure." Tori left the nurse's station as Leona took the call.

"This is Dr. Guillano," she said.

"Hey, Leona. It's Dr. Redding. I just wanted to let you know that little Bradly Carver has woken up. CPS has banned his foster parents from seeing him, at least for the time being, and I think he would feel better seeing a familiar face."

"That's amazing news!" Leona said. "Give me a few minutes and I'll be up." She dropped the phone into the receiver and hurried to the stockroom where she had last seen Bella.

Bella looked up when Leona burst through the door. "Just finishing up here, then I'm off duty. But if you needed something…"

"I just got off the phone with Dr. Redding from the ICU. He tells me that Brad is awake. I thought you'd want to see him before you go."

"What?" Bella squealed. She stood up and threw her arms around Leona. Leona instinctively wrapped her arms around her, and they held onto the embrace, both emotional about the news. She was excited to see Brad awake, as was Bella. It felt like he'd been unconscious for too long.

Slowly Bella pulled her arms down from the embrace. "I…I'm sorry," Bella said.

Leona shook her head. "Don't apologize. It's great news. You wanna go?"

"Um, yeah. Let me get clocked out and then I'll meet you at his room."

Leona nodded and left the room. As Bella brushed past her,

Leona stared at her backside, her mind racing. Just the feel of Bella's arms around her left her wanting more. She shivered, trying mentally to shake that feeling. She knew too well how much she wanted to keep that feeling going, but for so many reasons, she was forced to ignore the inner heat that coursed through her body.

She took the elevator up to the pediatric ICU. Leona waited just outside Brad's door, not wanting to see Brad before Bella had a chance to get to the room. Ten minutes later, Bella got off the elevator. She was dressed in a skirt and low-cut blouse. She wore a blazer over the blouse, but it didn't hide the cleavage that stared Leona straight in the face. Leona quickly looked away, willing her lips to not quiver. Why was Bella dressed like that? And would Leona ever have the opportunity to see her dressed so provocatively again?

She let her eyes lift long enough to brush over Bella's breasts and then to her eyes. "You're dressed, um…" Her words died and Bella tilted her head.

"Dressed um, what?" Bella asked.

Leona shrugged. "Just not used to seeing you in anything but scrubs. That's all."

"Do I not look okay?" Bella asked; her eyes dipped down to her cleavage and Leona was forced to follow Bella's gaze. Her breath hitched, and she mentally groaned. *Stop it, Leona. It will only cause you heartache.*

"You look great," Leona said, then bit down on her tongue. "I mean, you look fine. We should get in there so you can go wherever you need to go. It's obviously not anywhere in the hospital," Leona mumbled, pushing through to Brad's room.

Brad was seated in his bed and already looked a million times better even with the swelling and the oxygen coming out through his nose. "Hello, Brad." Bella smiled brightly. "Do you remember us?"

His eyes lit up, and he nodded. "Bella and Lona," he said.

Leona laughed. "Close enough." She reached out and ruffled her fingers through his hair. "How do you feel?"

He frowned. "Sore." He winced and touched his head.

"That will be something you'll be feeling for a few days," Leona reluctantly told him. "But before you know it, you'll be ready to jump right out of this bed."

"And ride my bike outside?" he asked, his eyes lit up.

Bella tossed a look over to Leona and Leona smirked. "If that's what you want," Leona answered.

Bella grabbed a chair and pulled it up to his bed. "Do you remember much of what happened?" she asked.

He frowned and shook his head. "They said I was hit by a car, but I don't remember."

"That's all right," Bella said. "You might get your memory back at some point."

"And if you don't," Leona continued, "that's all right, too."

Bella nodded in agreement. The door opened and Leona heard footsteps behind them. She turned and saw a woman entering the room. The woman smiled and approached the bed.

"Candice Gordon," she said in greeting, holding her hand out to Leona and then Bella.

"I'm Bella and this is Leona—Dr. Guillano. We're the nurse and doctor that helped Brad when he was here at the beginning of the month," Bella explained.

"Yes, I have you down on my list. I'm the social worker here in Chicago that will be helping Brad while he's in the system, which, unfortunately, he'll be going back into once he leaves the hospital."

Leona looked over at Brad; his eyes were slightly closed. "Hey buddy, you should try to get some rest. We'll be in later to see you." She looked over at Bella, who nodded.

"Goodbye for now," Bella said, leaning in and kissing his forehead. "Rest well."

"Thank you Bella and Lona." Brad yawned and shifted in the bed as Bella moved to Leona's side.

"May we speak to you for a moment out in the hall?" Leona asked.

Candice nodded, and the three of them left his room. It was Leona who was first to speak once the door was closed. "I'm assuming that his foster parents are out of the picture?"

Candice smiled gently. "With all due respect, I can't explain the case to you. I can just say that we're making sure we're doing what we can to keep that little boy safe."

"And we appreciate that," Bella said.

Leona looked over at Bella and they met each other's gaze. There was a smile on Bella's lips that made Leona respond with the same. Somehow this connection between the two of them had suddenly become much more magnetic.

"I should get back in to be with him. He's in good hands, I can assure you."

"Thank you, Ms. Gordon," Leona replied, turning her attention back to the social worker.

"It's just Candice," she said with a smile before going back into Brad's room.

Leona turned back to Bella. "Well, it's good to see that he appears to be doing well."

"The best news ever," Bella replied. She looked down at her watch and winced. "I'm going to be late," she said, looking back up to Leona.

It was obvious she was ready to head out on a hot date with her boyfriend. Leona wouldn't lie and say she wasn't jealous, but she wasn't going to show that. "Enjoy your night, Bella."

"Thank you. I'll be seeing you." Bella gave a slight wave and headed to the elevator.

Because Leona didn't want to get stuck on the elevator with Bella, she settled on using the stairs. She took a leisurely walk down the steps, her thoughts getting locking onto Bella. She caught herself smiling as those thoughts floated through her mind. She hesitated at the door to the pediatric floor and stood there, clutching the handle. If she ever caught herself hugging Bella again, she didn't think she would be able to pull herself away. She would have to make sure that didn't happen.

She opened the door and stepped into the corridor of the ward. As she rounded the corner, Jacqueline looked up and immediately waved her over. She released a huge sigh as Leona reached her.

"I wasn't sure where you were and the desk is swamped and Dr. Whalen has me..." She stopped and took a breath as Leona gawked at her. "Sorry, you have a phone call." She thrust it out in front of her and Leona smiled.

"Thanks, Jacqueline."

Jacqueline was a bit too flighty for Leona's liking. It was another reason why she had chosen Bella as her mentee. It was obvious, though, that the main reason was the attraction that Leona felt for Bella.

"Hello?"

The line seemed dead as Leona pulled the phone away from her ear and stared at it, like it would miraculously tell her who was on the other end. She put the phone back to her ear.

"*Hello?*" She spoke again.

"Leona?"

Leona fell against the counter. She clutched the phone tightly between her fingers so that she wouldn't drop it. "Why are you calling me? How'd you find me?"

"I, I, you see…"

Leona's breath hitched as she continued clinging to the phone.

"I tried every hospital. I didn't think I would ever be able to reach you. Yet here you are."

"Here I am, wondering why you're calling me. The way we left things…" Leona released a breath. "You aren't supposed to be calling me."

"I miss you, Le. Don't you miss me?"

Leona shook her head, angered by how Cicily apparently felt it was fine just to reach out because she thought Leona missed her. They had broken up. It was supposed to be a clean break.

"I'm not ready to talk to you."

"I said I'm sorry. Doesn't that account for anything?"

It'd been three months since Leona walked away from New York and left that life behind her. That included walking away from Cicily, the one woman she thought she might settle down with. Now, getting this call from her, Leona was reminded how much pain and anger she felt toward this woman. Cicily hadn't crossed her mind even once in the past three months, other than in the periphery, when Leona thought about how grateful she was to have a clean break. While there were still some complicated, residual feelings, Leona wouldn't tell her she missed her and give Cicily false hope.

"I've forgiven you, Cicily. Even before you asked for it. But I see things clearly, and what we had wasn't forever. I'm moving on and I suggest you do the same."

"Leona!" Cicily argued.

It pained Leona to hang up when she heard the way Cicily's voice broke. She didn't want to hurt her, but the sooner Cicily knew she wasn't holding onto their relationship, the better off Cicily would be. She turned to Jacqueline.

"If she calls again, tell her I'm not here."

Jacqueline nodded, her eyes wide.

This call was actually what Leona needed, to know she was on the right track and there was only one woman who occupied her thoughts day and night. Unfortunately, that woman wasn't available. That was the pain that hurt the most. So until then, Leona would just have to find a way to get over Bella Strong.

CHAPTER EIGHT

Bella

Bella rushed into the restaurant. She was sure she was going to be late and have to apologize repeatedly to Jackson for not being there, but she made it with two minutes to spare. Spotting Jackson at a nearby table, she waved and rushed up to him.

"I thought I wouldn't make it on time," Bella said.

Jackson stood and pulled her into his arms, kissing her with a hunger that took her by surprise. She froze, doing her best to kiss him back, but not feeling the same intensity.

She finally pressed her hand against his chest. "That was a warm welcome," she said.

"That's what happens when I miss you," he replied.

She blushed and took a seat, letting the weight release from her chest. "It's good to be sitting down. Today was a rough day," Bella said. She smiled and added, "It got better as I was about to clock out."

"You knew you were coming to see me?" Jackson asked, a teasing grin on his lips.

"Well, that, and you know that foster boy I told you about who got hit by a car?"

Jackson nodded, then took a sip of his water.

Bella beamed. "He woke up today. He's going to be fine."

"That's great news, babe," he said. "Oh, and by the way, we're not going to be dining alone tonight."

Bella frowned and turned around to look where his eyes had wandered. Her jaw dropped as her mom, dad, and sister approached the table. "Mom? Dad? Veronica?"

She jumped up and hugged each of them, surprised and confused why they were there. They were all smiles, but when she looked over to Jackson, she saw that his grin was the biggest. "What's going on?" she asked.

"Can't your family just want to come see you?" her mom asked. "It's been forever. Or at least feels like it's been forever."

Her mother's grin widened, and Bella had to admit it was good to see all of them, even if she had been kept out of the loop. It wasn't like Jackson to take the initiative to do something like this. His wide smile showed that he was proud of himself.

"I'm just happy to see you all," Bella admitted. They sat down and she grinned and shook her head. "I should have known something was up, since we're at a larger table. You're so sneaky, Jackson." She reached out and touched his arm.

As she touched him, Bella realized again that she didn't feel the same spark she had felt when she had hugged Leona earlier. When she and Jackson had kissed moments ago, there had been this deep passion in their embrace that had come from him, but she hadn't felt the chemistry pouring from them like she had around Leona. That struck her to her core. What in the world was wrong with her? Jackson was part of her plan, not Leona. She brought her hand back and proceeded to look down at her menu, trying not to let her unsettled feelings distract her from an evening with her family.

After they ordered, Veronica, her parents, and Jackson got caught up in conversation, with Jackson focusing his attention on her sister. Veronica was just talking about cheerleading and a book report, but Jackson acted as if Veronica was talking about the most thrilling things. He seemed intrigued by it all. Seeing him like that couldn't help but put a smile on Bella's lips.

Jackson was a good man by anyone's standards. When they got married, she would be the luckiest woman in the world. When had that wound up not being enough?

"What are you thinking about, honey?"

She jerked when her mother reached out and touched her arm. She turned and looked at her, then gave a slight shrug. "Nothing. Everything." Bella smirked. "You probably know more than anyone what I'm going through. Tired and not sure which way is right and which is left."

Bella reached out and grabbed her glass of water. She held onto it for a moment, suddenly feeling overwhelmed.

"I'm sure it's extremely intense," Bella's mom said. "But you have to remember, I didn't have to worry about school. I had already graduated when I started working at a hospital. You're ahead of the game. It's exciting, though, right?"

Bella nodded. "And overwhelming," she whispered. Her mother squeezed her hand.

"It will get better. Trust me on that." Her quiet words were meant to reassure Bella, and Bella wished she could believe them.

The waitress brought them their food and Bella spent time just focusing on eating and not making small talk. She looked up when she noticed there was a lull at the table.

"So, Veronica..." Bella started. "How's school going?"

Her sister groaned and scrunched up her face. "Depends on what part of school you're referring to," she said. "Classes? Ugh!" Her sister dipped a fry into her ketchup. "As I was telling Jackson, the highlight has been cheerleading, and this summer I plan on going to cheerleading camp." Her eyes lit up.

"That's cool. But you know, school is really where you need to make sure you keep your grades up. If they fall, then the pyramid will tumble, because you won't be there to hold it up."

Veronica nodded. "That's what Mom keeps saying." She rolled her eyes. "But really…What am I going to need all this math mumbo jumbo for?"

Bella laughed. "When you're done with school, where do you see yourself? I mean, when you go off to college."

Veronica shrugged. "I thought maybe I would be a vet tech or something. I love animals."

Bella waved her finger. "And that's exactly why you'll need math—calculations for medicine, or even at the register. I wouldn't count out your education just yet. Down the road you may see that you were way off in your calculations."

Veronica smirked. "I see what you did there." She shrugged. "I'm doing my best to keep my grades up. I study every night and I do like most of my classes."

"That's good to hear," Bella said.

The table went quiet as they all enjoyed their food. Before Bella knew it, Veronica and Jackson were talking about other small topics. Bella appreciated being able to just listen and not have to participate in the conversation. But in that small time frame, her mind wandered back to Leona. She wondered what she was doing at that very moment. Possibly still at the hospital.

"Honey…" Jackson reached out and touched her arm. She jerked and looked over at him.

His eyebrows furrowed. "You look like you've seen a ghost." He laughed. "I was talking to you and you looked like you were somewhere far away."

I was. And with another woman.

"Sorry." Her face flushed, and she touched her cheek. It was warm. "What were you saying?"

"Just that it was good everyone was able to get together tonight."

Bella smiled and nodded. "All thanks to you," she replied.

He slipped his fingers around hers and squeezed her hand, then looked around the table as Bella's eyes dropped to their intertwined hands. Bella's mom cleared her throat and Bella looked over to her. Her eyes narrowed and she arched an eyebrow at her daughter.

Bella forced a smile onto her face. "It was great to see you all," she said, and she meant it.

"Let's just hope we're able to get together again before too much time has passed," her dad commented, and everyone agreed.

Ten minutes later, they were all outside the restaurant and hugging one another, giving their goodbyes. "Love you, Mom," Bella said, hugging her tighter.

When she started to pull away, her mother rested her lips to her ear. "I think you need to talk to Jackson," she whispered.

Bella frowned and looked at her, and her mom gave a weak smile. At that moment, Bella knew her mother completely seen through her during their time together. She wondered how much her mother had figured out. She wasn't ready to have any deep conversation with Jackson, either easy or hard. She couldn't. It would throw everything off. She just needed to concentrate again on what she wanted out of life and stop thinking about Leona.

"Love you all," Bella called, waving at her family as she and Jackson turned away and headed toward her car.

"I'm parked over here, too," he said, pointing.

"Yeah, I saw your car when I got here," Bella replied.

When they reached her car, she turned to him. "Tonight was nice. Thanks for thinking of it."

He grinned. "I'm glad you enjoyed it."

He wrapped his arm around her and pulled her to him. As they kissed, she felt the hunger coming from him, and she pressed her hand against his chest, ending the kiss. It wound up a bit awkward, but she thought about what her mother had just said to her. She always knew Jackson felt stronger emotions for her than she did for him, and she figured that would grow with time and dedication to their marriage. But after experiencing that intense spark with Leona, something she'd never experienced before, nothing felt right anymore. Life with Jackson didn't feel right, and that was a huge problem.

"I should head home," she said.

"I could follow you," he offered, a teasing grin on his lips. "After all, I'm not ready for the night to end. Are you?"

Her jaw clenched, and she quickly searched for reasons she couldn't have him coming back to her place. She opened her mouth and released a yawn. He frowned. "I'm sorry. I'm just so tired. I wouldn't be the best company tonight."

He nodded. "I understand. There's always another day." He kissed her softly and she let it linger so her feelings wouldn't be conspicuous. "Love you."

"Me, too," she said.

She opened her car door and looked over her shoulder. He stood with one hand holding onto her door, waiting for her to climb into the car. She paused, opening her mouth to possibly explain where her head was, but no words would come. Instead, she said, "See you," waving and quickly sliding into her car.

As she drove away from him, Bella's heart broke a little. Stringing him along wasn't the right thing to do, but telling him that it was over was even harder. How could she just let go of the vision she'd had for her life for so many years?

———

BELLA'S MIND WAS TOO FOGGY TO GO HOME, AND SHE DIDN'T want to be alone with her thoughts. Thankfully, she didn't have any early classes, so she decided to stay out a little longer and go somewhere familiar with lots of activity. Anything to distract herself from the mess her life was becoming.

She drove to a small cafe near Capmed, one she sometimes stopped in for a quick bite to eat before and after her shifts. The staff there was chatty, so maybe they could help ease her mind with some kind of gossip or general small talk. As she pushed open the door to the bustling interior, though, her gaze immediately zeroed in on a familiar face. Leona.

She was sitting on a stool at the counter, sipping from a mug and reading a book. Bella thought of leaving, but before she could, Leona looked up, as if she had a sixth sense that had told her Bella had entered. Bella forced a weak smile, waved, and then joined Leona at the counter.

"Hey," Bella said, feeling awkward.

Leona smiled, her eyes warm and inviting. She had a vulnerability to her that Bella didn't see when they were at work. "Hi. I just got off shift and thought I'd grab some hot chocolate and do some reading to help me relax. Stressful day. Somehow, being in a busy atmosphere helps me unwind more than being at home alone."

Bella nodded and relaxed as her eyes darted over the casual jeans and shirt Leona wore. Meeting her outside the hospital like this was so different, and it sent a thrill through her. "Me, too. I've had so much on my mind, places like this always help."

They sat in silence for a few moments, both lost in their own thoughts. Bella ordered some tea, wondering if she should say something or just let Leona keep reading. Before she could make a decision, Leona spoke up.

"How was your evening out?" she asked, not looking up from her book.

Bella tensed. "It was...fine."

Leona glanced up, eyebrows raised. "Just 'fine'?"

Bella shrugged. The server brought her tea, and she mindlessly stirred it with a spoon. "Yeah. I mean, we had a nice time and all, but...I don't know. I guess I just haven't been feeling it lately."

"Are you talking about your boyfriend?"

Bella nodded.

"Well, I'm a good listener."

Bella hesitated. Was it okay to be sitting here telling Leona about her life? Leona was her superior, so shouldn't they maintain certain boundaries? There was also the whole feelings situation.

"I understand if you don't feel like sharing," Leona said when Bella didn't respond. She looked a bit sad, which tugged at Bella's heartstrings. Leona really cared about listening to her vent?

Bella gave in and let everything out. She told Leona about Jackson and her life plan and how uncertain she was feeling lately about all of her choices.

Leona nodded slowly throughout Bella's rambling as if she understood exactly what Bella was going through. When Bella finally finished with a sigh and sipped her tea, Leona said softly, "Sounds like you're dealing with a lot. I know how you feel."

Bella looked up at her, surprised. "You do?"

Leona nodded again and gave her a small, sad smile. "Yeah. I've experienced my share of uncertainty in my life as well as relationship problems." She reached out to touch Bella's hand. "Just know that you're not alone."

Bella didn't move her hand, letting Leona's touch linger and letting her words sink in. Bella felt a sudden wave of comfort wash over her. It was nice to know she wasn't alone in feeling this way.

"So what did you do?" Bella asked. "How did you deal with the uncertainty and your past relationships?"

Leona shrugged and took a sip of her drink before answering. "I guess I just decided that I deserved better," she said simply. "I deserve to be with someone who ignites something strong and beautiful within me. Life is too short to settle, which sounds like what you're doing. Forgive me for being bold, but you don't have to stick to your plan if what you want starts to change. It's okay to take chances and go after what truly fulfills you in life. Sometimes what we need turns out to be different from what we wanted."

Bella nodded, understanding. She had been feeling the same way lately, but hearing it from someone else made it feel more real. More possible.

"Thank you," Bella said quietly. "For talking to me, I mean. It means a lot."

"Don't mention it," Leona said. "That's what friends are for."

Friends. The word echoed in Bella's mind. "You really see us that way? As equals?"

"Of course. I know we work together, but we're not at work now, are we?"

Bella grinned, her first genuine grin that entire evening. "I'm so relieved. I've felt a lot of pressure to live up to your expectations. You're my superior, so I do feel a bit awkward right now talking about my life so much, but...I also admire your confidence and like your company."

She blushed and looked away. Leona had gotten her to open up, but now she might be overstepping and letting too much out.

Leona hesitated and then touched Bella's hand again. "I enjoy your company, too. I hope that, moving forward, you can see us more as equals at work. I want to mentor you, but that doesn't mean I'm your superior. Just a friend trying to help you out, okay?"

Bella nodded, moving away from Leona's touch to lift her mug. Heat had spread through her entire body and the cafe had suddenly become *very* stuffy. But Leona wanted to be friends, not something more.

They spent some more time together chatting about lighter topics, and soon Bella felt too tired to keep the conversation going. She really needed a good night's sleep and to process everything that had happened that evening. Driving home, she thought about her conversation with Leona. At least she had someone who understood what she was going through and could offer some advice. For the first time in a long time, Bella felt hopeful. Maybe things were finally going to start looking up.

———

BELLA TAPPED LIGHTLY ON BRAD'S DOOR. "COME IN," Kandice's voice rang out. Kandice was a social worker and Bella was glad Brad had someone who was going to uphold her promise of keeping him safe.

"Hey, Bella," Kandice greeted her. "Just in time."

"I am?" Bella asked.

Kandice nodded. "I have a meeting with a possible foster for Brad. I didn't want him to wake up and not find anyone here, so I didn't want to leave him alone. He had a painful night."

She then registered that Bella was in her scrubs. "Oh, silly me, you're probably here for work. I guess you won't be able to stick around in case he wakes. That's fine; I'll just let the nurses know."

"I have an hour or so. Thought I would just check up on my favorite patient." Bella looked over to Brad, who was sleeping soundly. "But you say you have a possible foster lined up for him?"

She nodded. "A couple, actually. They don't have any children but are looking to foster. They live about two minutes from here and I'm doing a house call. It won't be long. If I'm not back, just let the staff know."

"Okay. Sounds good. See you, Kandice." Bella sat down in a chair next to the bed. She looked over at Brad, noticing the slight smile on his lips. Bella reached out and touched the wisp of curl that hung at his eyes. When she pulled her hand back, she felt a slight pain in her chest. The thought of Brad leaving the hospital and going to live with another family bothered her. She wanted to make sure she got to see him again. But right now, there was little guarantee.

Bella fell back in her seat and watched Brad's chest slowly rise and fall as he slept so soundly. He had been improving greatly over the last week and it was a relief to everyone. His bones were healing nicely and his external wounds were slowly fading. Bella just hoped whatever family got to raise Brad would keep him safe and that he wouldn't have any reason to stay in the hospital again.

Bella had been watching over Brad for twenty minutes when he slowly rustled himself awake. He shifted onto his left side and opened his eyes. A smile broadened on his face. "Bella," he said happily.

"Hey, bud." Bella got up and helped him sit up. He held out his arms, and she hugged him tightly. "How are you feeling?"

"Good!" He nodded eagerly. "Do you know when I'll be able to get out of here?" There was a slight frown etched on his forehead.

"Well, I think they just want to make sure you're stronger first. While you appear strong on the outside, they need to ensure you aren't having any problems. Do you understand?"

He nodded, but then shook his head. "I'm okay. I just want to go home," he whined, his young age showing. Bella's heart ached for the boy, imaging how confusing it all must have been for him.

"I know you do." She looked down at her watch. Time was slowly ticking by. "You wanna go for a walk?" she asked.

His eyes widened, and he nodded vigorously. She held up her hand and then quickly disappeared out of his room. "Hey, Jess," she said. "Would it be all right if I just pushed Brad around the hospital for a minute? He's anxious to get out of his room."

She smiled and nodded. "That'd be great. I'll get you a wheel-chair." A few seconds later, she returned with a chair.

"Thanks." Bella went back into the room, where Brad was already sitting on the edge of his bed. He groaned. "You said we were gonna take a walk."

Bella laughed. "Sorry. I'll walk, you'll ride. It's best this way."

He grumbled but allowed Bella to help him into the chair. She pushed him out of the room and straight to the elevator.

"Where are we going?" Brad asked, his eyes still bright.

"You'll see," she said mysteriously. She grabbed a blanket from a shelf and placed it over him. "Just in case you get a chill." Bella pushed the button to call the elevator and they waited for it to reach their floor.

"It's taking forever," Brad mumbled.

Bella smirked. "Good things come to those who wait."

When the doors opened, Leona stood there, leaning against the wall of the elevator. She straightened up when she saw them. "Hey," she said.

Bella's heart fluttered. "Hi."

"Lona," Brad said. "We're going for a walk. Wanna come?"

"I'd love to," Leona said with a smile.

Bella looked down, one thought immediately coming to mind. *Good things come to those who wait.*

CHAPTER NINE

Leona

L ater that day, Leona rounded the corner and spotted
Bella at the nurses' station. Her head was resting against
her hand and her eyes were closed. It was a quiet evening,
so no one was pressing Bella to take care of patients' needs, but
Leona laughed to herself. Never had she caught a nurse napping on
the job. But Bella was something special, and she worked so hard.

Really, Leona wasn't surprised to find her napping. She had
noticed how exhausted Bella had looked when they had been on
their walk earlier. Speaking of the walk, she hadn't expected to
enjoy the silence so much. It had felt like they were just out on a
stroll, with no cares in the world. For a moment, it had even felt
like they were a family. Leona had longed for a family for so many
years, she had just let herself fall into the moment and simply
enjoy the fantasy.

When she'd first met Bella, their age difference had stared her
right in the face. But as she grew closer to Bella and got to know

her, she found that the gap no longer mattered. She saw how determined and hardworking Bella was, and how she always pushed through despite any setbacks or errors.

Bella had a lot of resilience despite doubting herself so much. And she had such a kind, caring heart that Leona knew she'd make a great mother one day. Thanks to their unexpected meeting at the cafe a few days ago, Leona now knew that motherhood was something Bella wanted and had already planned for. It made Leona's feelings for her grow. Now she was getting into riskier territory, especially since Bella was questioning her relationship with her boyfriend.

Leona had loved the walk and the feeling that this could be her family, or that she could have something similar in the future. Did she want that with Bella? When the walk had ended, Leona had dismissed those thoughts. Just because Bella was on uncertain ground with her boyfriend didn't mean she was interested in women, or older women. Or Leona.

She stepped up to the desk where Bella was napping, hating to wake her up. She looked so peaceful. But at any moment, someone else could round the corner, like Tori or a head of the hospital. Either way, it wouldn't look good if someone else happened to catch Bella asleep.

Leona lightly cleared her throat. When that didn't jar her awake, she tapped her on the shoulder.

"Bella!" she whispered.

Bella's eyes flew open, and she jumped up from her chair. "Was I asleep?" she asked, her eyes wide and her cheeks flushed.

"It's fine. You obviously needed the rest," Leona pointed out.

Bella looked away from her, her eyes hazy as she quickly shook her head. "That's so embarrassing. It's not fine. You're my boss and…"

"Whoa, slow down," Leona said, reaching out for her arm.

Bella dropped her gaze to her hand, grasped around Bella's arm, and Leona slowly pulled it back. "I'm not going to tell anyone. As far as I can tell, I'm the only one who saw. No harm, no foul." She threw up her arms. "I swear."

Bella looked up and frowned. "But why? Shouldn't I be written up or something? This can't possibly be all right." Her eyes were still bugging out.

That was true. But Leona wasn't going to report her. She knew how hard Bella worked.

"You want to be written up? I can get the chief of staff right now. Your call." Leona pretended to turn away, but Bella was quick to reply.

"Well, no, but…" Leona grinned and turned back around, and Bella chuckled in relief. "You were teasing. Of course you were."

"It's really all right, Bella. It could happen to anyone." Leona hesitated and scrunched up her face in thought. "Although, I do worry you're pushing yourself too much. Maybe you should go take your break."

"But it's not time," Bella argued, looking down at her watch.

"There are no set break times," Leona replied. "You could freshen up or take in a few more z's. Your call. I just think that you need to get off your feet."

"I guess you're right. I'll be back in ten." Bella turned to leave.

"Make it fifteen, Bella. Don't push yourself. If you do, you're liable to make yourself sick and that helps no one. Understood?"

Bella looked over her shoulder, holding Leona's gaze. Finally, she nodded, then went to the elevator. Once she was gone, Leona turned back to her list of patients she needed to follow up on. She entered a room where one of their oldest patients, seventeen-year-old Martina, lay. She had her eyes peeled on the TV screen, but when Leona entered, she groaned.

"Finally!" She turned, then rolled her eyes when she saw it was

Leona. "Thought you were Bella. She was supposed to get me ibuprofen like an hour ago. My arm is throbbing."

"She was detained," Leona quickly replied. "I'll go grab you something." She turned and left her room, then walked to the medicine cabinet.

"Have you seen Bella?" Jacqueline asked, coming out of a room.

"She's on break," Leona replied, putting the pills into a cup and grabbing an extra bottle of water. "You need something?"

Jacqueline hesitated. "Well, you're the doctor and this is trivial, so I guess I'll just do it. But I have Dr. Whalen waiting and really shouldn't detain him…"

"It's fine, Jacqueline," Leona cut in. "I don't mind. What do you need with Bella?"

"Tommy was supposed to be taken down to CT twenty minutes ago. My patient is next and has been ready, but they're still waiting on Tommy."

Leona cringed. That wasn't good, but with the way Bella was feeling, she felt compelled to support her. "That's my fault. I put Bella on a project and told her I would move the schedule to accommodate it. I'm sorry."

Jacqueline tilted her head and shrugged. "It happens."

"I'll call down to radiology and tell them we're moving your patient in front of ours. Thanks for the heads-up."

Leona turned away from her and hurried back to Martina's room. "Here you go." She handed over the cup and water and waited for Martina to take her medicine. "Need anything else? How are you feeling?"

"Pretty good, other than the pain. Thanks!" Martina turned back to her TV and Leona slipped out of her room. She went over to the receptionist's desk and called down to the radiology department.

"This is Pete."

"Hey, Pete. It's Dr. Guillano. There's been a misunderstanding. We're moving Dr. Whalen's patient in front of mine. Call the floor once you're ready for us."

"Sounds good. Thanks for the update."

Pete hung up and Leona leaned against the desk and sighed. She glanced at her watch and frowned. It'd already been twenty minutes since she sent Bella on her fifteen-minute break. She went to the elevator and took it down to the breakroom.

When she entered the room, she stopped. Bella sat at the only occupied table. Her head was down and she looked completely knocked out. Leona cleared her throat, which jogged Bella awake. "Where am I?" Bella asked, jumping up.

"Bella, look at me." Leona knelt in front of her. Bella's eyes slowly refocused on Leona. "You're exhausted. You need one night off where you don't have work and you don't have school. You need to go home."

"I can't," she argued, shaking her head. "I'll get a coffee and be fine."

"You're not fine, Bella. I'll cover for you. You go home and get some sleep. And this isn't a request. It's an order." Bella frowned and looked down at her clenched hands. "You'll be fine. I promise."

Finally, Bella nodded. "Thank you."

"Just get that rest so tomorrow you'll be better. Take care." Leona left her in the breakroom and headed back to the elevator. When the elevator doors opened, she saw Kandice, who looked up and greeted Leona.

"Hey," Leona said in greeting. "Headed out for the evening?"

"Yeah, Brad is resting and in good hands tonight. I hear he could be ready to leave the hospital by next week. Great news considering I think I found the perfect foster parents for him."

"Oh really?" Leona asked, her chest heavy. "Bella did mention you have a prospective couple. Are you sure you've given it plenty of thought? I would hate for him to get involved with another couple incapable of handling his care."

She smiled. "I appreciate your concern. Both you and Bella have been great for Brad and I've appreciated both of you worrying about the little guy, but I'm confident. This family has no kids, but they have a dog and are looking to expand their family. Unfortunately, they can't have a child of their own. So, there's potential they could adopt him in the end. That's what we all want, right?"

Leona nodded, but she was sorry to think that Brad would soon leave the hospital. Who knows when they would see him again? "That sounds good then. He's a lucky guy."

"He will be," Kandice said. "His life hasn't been so lucky, so he deserves this. Anyway, I should head out. See you later, Leona."

Kandice waved and Leona watched her go. There was still a knot that rested in her gut. In a short amount of time, she had gotten attached to Brad. She wanted a family, and that was more obvious to her now. Hopefully she'd have that one day soon.

The thing is, Brad wasn't the only one she had gotten attached to.

———

LEONA SIGHED AS SHE STARED AT HER CELLPHONE. *JUST CALL her. You'll feel much better if you do.* After staring at the phone for what felt like forever, she finally pressed the number in her contact list. There went nothing. She just hoped she wouldn't be seen as a stalker when she was merely trying to be thoughtful. She quickly hung up the phone before it could ring. Leona cringed, hoping Bella's phone didn't get a notification.

Leona fell back in her seat and stared at her phone again. She was being a chicken, but why? After several more minutes, she grabbed her phone again and hit the Call button. The line started ringing, and it was too late to hang up again. She had to go through with the call.

"Hello?"

"Uh, hey, Bella. This is Le…Leona. Are you busy?"

"Um, hey."

There was some hesitancy behind that greeting, and Leona waited for the tension to break, but it felt even more awkward as the seconds ticked on without either of them speaking.

Bella broke the silence. "How'd you get my number?"

Not exactly what Leona was hoping she'd say.

"Well, since you have a landline, one search and pulled it right up." Leona laughed nervously. "I hope that's okay. Don't want to give you stalker vibes or anything."

"Well, no, it's fine. Just surprised to get a call from you on my home number. That's all."

"I honestly wasn't sure I'd reach you. I thought maybe you'd have school or something this morning. But I'm glad to chat you up." Leona cringed again. *Chat you up?* Who even talked like that?

"Anyway, the reason I'm calling is that I just wanted to check up on you. You know, given the way you were last night. You were so tired and all. I wanted to make sure you made it home and got plenty of rest."

There, that seemed like a sufficient explanation.

There was a pause, then Bella said, "Oh, well, that's sweet of you."

Leona smiled and sat down in the nearest chair. That was a good sign. She found it sweet and not the least bit stalkerish. "I'm a doctor. It's my job to care."

An exhale sounded on the other end of the line, and Leona opened her mouth to say that it didn't come out at all how she wanted it to. It seemed crass, like she was saying she only cared because she was a doctor. It wasn't genuine and frankly the furthest thing from the truth. "I mean…"

"I get what you mean," Bella replied, interrupting her. "And it makes perfect sense. In the profession you're in, you're expected to care. So, thank you for doing your job well. Anyway, I have to go. I have laundry and a million other things to do. Thanks for calling, Leona—or, I should say, Dr. Guillano."

"Wait, Bella, that came out all wrong, really. Yes, I'm a doctor. That fact is very true and can't be changed. But it isn't the only reason I called. I was concerned about you, not as my nurse, but as a friend. I just didn't want you to hang up thinking that I was merely calling because I felt it was out of duty or something. That would be the furthest thing from the truth."

There was a long silence and Leona leaned into the call, waiting, holding her breath, trying to hear any kind reaction on Bella's side, whether it was hesitation or warmth. She released a breath and waited some more.

"Are you there?" she finally asked.

"Yeah, I'm here. I get what you're saying. I just took it the wrong way. I do feel much better than I was last night. I'm rejuvenated and ready to go to work this evening."

Leona felt relieved to hear that. "That's great to hear."

"Yep. And I don't have classes today, so I plan on just laying low until tonight. I'm assuming you're on duty tonight?"

"Yeah, I'll be there at eight. What time do you come in?" Leona asked, settling into the smooth conversation between them.

"Also eight."

A thought came to Leona. "So, if you don't have anything else planned, would you like to grab a bite to eat before we go in?"

"You mean like in the cafeteria?" Bella asked.

Leona released a laugh, then bit down on her lower lip, not

expecting it to have come out as loud as it did. "Well, the cafeteria has good food and all, but I was thinking more along the lines of outside of the hospital. There's a seafood restaurant around the corner and I've been meaning to try it. Or, if that's not your thing, we can go somewhere else."

"I love seafood," Bella replied.

"Okay, then. Six o'clock?"

Belle immediately agreed and Leona hung up the phone, slightly taken aback by her own bold attitude. Was she pushing things too far? She was simply trying to be friendly. They could be friends despite her growing attraction—right?

Regardless, the only thing that mattered was that Bella had said yes, and while she couldn't go as far to say it was a date, she could say that she was excited about getting to know Bella a little more.

CHAPTER TEN

Bella

I t felt too close to an actual date, even though she showed up at the restaurant wearing scrubs. Ever since Leona had suggested grabbing a bite to eat, Bella couldn't stop thinking about what that would entail. What would they talk about? How would she feel? It frightened her in a way that startled her.

She arrived at the restaurant to find Leona already sitting down in one of the booths. Bella approached the table and Leona looked up and greeted her with a smile. She had a sincere look about her, one that completely fit a woman who had enough empathy to dig up her number and call to check up on her. She had jumped to the conclusion that Leona had only made the call because she was Bella's superior, but it wasn't a fair conclusion to jump to. Leona had said just as much, and they were friends. Or trying to be. Bella still felt a little awkward calling a superior that. But looking back, she was glad that Leona had explained herself. Otherwise, Bella would've kept thinking Leona was only calling out of duty, and Bella didn't think she'd be able to handle that.

"Hi there," Leona said, standing to her feet.

"This place has some of the best shrimp you'll ever find," Bella said. "If that's your thing."

"I'll keep that in mind. Thank you."

They both sat down, and Bella opened her menu and peered down at it, feeling Leona's eyes on her. When Bella looked up, Leona looked back down. It was something that was probably just in her mind, but it was like there was a way that Leona's eyes often followed her. She shook the thought from her mind. It was merely a coincidence, she was sure.

The waiter came to their table, and they ordered their drinks, followed promptly by their food. When he was gone, Bella looked across the table. Again, Leona's eyes were dancing.

Leona cleared her throat and sat up straighter. "So, I ran into Kandice last night. It was shortly after I sent you home."

"Oh yeah? Did she say how Brad's doing?"

"He's doing well—well enough that he should be discharged soon. She said sometime next week, by the looks of things." Bella nodded, happy for Brad.

It was great news, but Bella needed to know the whole story. Leona continued, "She said that there's this couple that is super excited about fostering him, possibly even fostering to adopt. And she said that they're good people. That's promising."

Bella nodded again and looked down at the empty spot in front of her. If it all sounded good, which it did, then why did she feel this sadness radiating through her body?

"You don't look too happy," Leona observed.

"I'm happy for him. I'm sad for me." Bella let out a sigh. "I mean, I feel like I've known him a while and I just hate the fact that after he leaves the hospital, we might lose contact completely."

Leona's expression fell. "I had the same thought. So, I would say it's sad for us."

Bella liked knowing there was someone else concerned about the little guy, someone that she could talk to about Brad. She liked that she didn't have to worry about droning on about something she couldn't change to someone else.

Leona continued. "The funny thing is, I even considered looking into fostering. I would have said something to Kandice, but it seems like everything has already been figured out." She shrugged. "As long as he's happy."

Bella perked up. She was touched that Leona would have even considered fostering Brad. If Bella had one ounce of time, then maybe she would have as well. But there just wasn't any time with school and work and trying to maintain her relationship with Jackson.

Leona smiled at her, eyes playful. "What are you grinning about?"

Bella touched her cheeks. She had been grinning like a fool at Leona. She laughed at herself. "Oh, sorry. I just...Well, there's this softer side of you that I'm seeing more of. You're always so confident and self-assured, and a little firm at work, but you also have this soft spot. Considering how you've encouraged me, I know you'll be a wonderful mother." She bit her lip. It felt rude to pry into it too much, but she was curious about Leona's past.

Leona blushed and avoided eye contact. "Thank you, Bella."

"So, why—"

She was interrupted by the server bringing their food. After poking around her plate a bit, she found the nerve to try again. "Why did things never work out for you?"

"You mean motherhood?"

Bella nodded.

Leona let out a long sigh, as if she'd been holding it in for years. "The wrong partners, I guess. I settled, just like I told you to be careful to not do. I know how it feels to think you have limited options, but I can tell you from experience that there's a big world out there and sometimes life takes you in different directions. My last relationship was a disaster, so I moved here for a fresh start. I don't think my body can handle a pregnancy anymore, and it was tough to come to terms with that, but fostering can help a child already in this world who needs a stable, loving home. I've decided I can do it on my own."

Bella touched her chest. "That's so amazing you would do that. And I'm sorry things didn't work out. Men are tricky, aren't they?"

"Women."

Bella almost choked on her food. "What?"

Leona gulped water and then said, "My past relationships have been with women."

Bella stared, even though she didn't mean to and knew it was probably rude. Leona's admission sent her insides whirling. If Leona was interested in women, that changed so much—mostly, Bella's chances with her. But that was silly to think of, because Leona wasn't interested in Bella in that way. Right?

"Oh," Bella said. "That's...I'm sorry for assuming. I guess relationships are just tricky period, no matter who you're with."

Leona nodded silently and focused on her food.

Thankfully, their conversation turned to work.

As Bella ate and the conversation got easier between them, Bella became more assured about speaking her mind instead of being hesitant to say things she wanted to say.

"Can I ask you something?" Bella asked halfway through the meal.

Leona looked up, catching her eye before dropping her fork. "I'm a little nervous as to what you're going to say, but ask away." She laughed, sipping on her water.

"When you gave me that evaluation, you said that I wasn't the type to have nurses' skills. Do you still feel that way?"

Leona set her napkin down on the table. "I didn't use those words. And I can honestly say that you *are* fit to be a nurse. I was concerned at the beginning, but after working with you, I'm confident you can do it. My concern now is that maybe you're pushing yourself too much. I've been in this field long enough to know when someone isn't giving themselves ample time to rest. And I believe I was right to think that."

"But I won't always have school and work trying to share equal time," Bella pointed out.

"You're very right in that aspect. But nursing is a gig that takes a lot of time and energy even if you don't have school. I just want to prepare you for that, as your mentor."

Leona smiled and went back to eating. "This food is delicious. This place might just be one of my top three restaurants so far."

Bella looked down at her food, not fully satisfied with Leona's response. She had danced around the question more than she had answered definitively.

"I'm dedicated," she said.

Leona looked up mid-bite and nodded. "I have no doubt you are. If you put the hard work in, then you'll make a fine nurse. But know that if it doesn't work out, that's all right, too. You have other options."

She continued to eat while Bella sat there, thinking about Leona's words. There wasn't any way Bella would let failure be an option.

Since they were so openly talking about things, more words flowed easily between the two of them. Bella realized how strong her interest in Leona had become. Though she wasn't going to act on it, she liked the idea of them being friends. But something still nagged at her. "Is this okay? Us hanging out together outside of work?"

Leona gave her a concerned look. "Of course. Why wouldn't it be?"

"I'm having trouble separating the fact that you're my boss at work but not my boss in this setting."

Instead of looking more concerned, Leona smiled. "You show a lot of maturity."

Bella's eyes shot to Leona. "I do?"

"Mm-hmm. You're sharing what's bothering you and not keeping it in. That's a level of maturity I don't always see in people my age. So many of my past relationships..." She stopped, clearing her throat and switching gears. "I can understand how you might be struggling. Instead of me being your boss, what if you think of it as us simply being on a team, trying to do what's best for each patient? We each have different skills and roles, and we work together for a greater cause. I know it may feel like I'm bossing you around, but I really don't want it to be like that. We're just communicating with each other about what needs to be done."

Bella considered her words a while and then finally nodded. Thinking of them as teammates helped a lot. "I like that idea."

They smiled at each other, their gazes lingering too long for two people who were supposed to be just friends.

They finished their meal, and Bella tried to enjoy her time with Leona and not worry about anything else. She knew Leona was trying to help by suggesting there were other options out there for Bella, like a different career and different future, but it still nagged at Bella's mind. She really didn't want to give up nursing, so she would continue to do her best. Outside of nursing, though, was she getting more comfortable with letting go of her life plan and considering a different future? That thought was both terrifying and thrilling.

———

THE ONLY TWO PEOPLE WORKING THE FLOOR THAT NIGHT were Bella and Leona. Luckily, they immediately got into their shift and Bella didn't have time to think too much about all of their recent interactions outside of work. And the doubts Leona still had about her. She knew Leona had only the best intentions, but it still hurt that she thought Bella was pushing herself too hard and needed to consider new options or take time off. Bella could handle anything and everything. She was capable. She wasn't a quitter, and she wouldn't fail.

"Bed four-zero-five needs a fresh bag of IV fluids rehung. Bed four-one-two needs a bath, and bed four-zero-eight needs his labs drawn." Bella nodded, jotting down the notes, feeling like a walking zombie, as she had been feeling the whole night. She just wanted Leona to look at her with confidence and say that she was handling everything and doing a stellar job. Was that too much to ask? "And four-five-zero needs a story read to him."

Bella frowned and looked up. "Huh?"

Leona smirked. "I was worried that you weren't paying attention." She leaned against the wall and arched an eyebrow. "Seems like ever since we got to work, you've been a tad distracted."

Bella shrugged. "Nothing I can't work out for myself. I'll get on this." She held up her notes and hurried about doing the tasks that Leona gave to her.

After getting through her tasks, Bella rounded a corner, spotting Leona coming out of another room. "What's next?" Bella asked. "Another bath? Another lab draw? Perhaps I really should read the patient in room four-five-zero a story."

Leona grabbed her hand and pulled her toward a closet as Bella resisted, digging her heels into the ground.

"What are you doing?" Bella asked as Leona shut the door

behind them. When Bella tried to reach for the handle, Leona slid into her path.

"No...What are you doing, Bella? What did I say this time to irk you? Because something has clearly messed with your mind. The sooner you tell me what it is, the better off we'll all be."

Bella crossed her arms, putting up an invisible barrier between them. Leona arched an eyebrow.

"Fine...I'm hurt, all right?"

Leona frowned. "Hurt? About what?"

Bella turned away from her, creating some distance. When she twirled back around, Leona was still looking at her. "Hurt that you still doubt that I can handle myself. You doubt my ability to juggle work and school. I'm surprised you haven't gone to the board and said that they should revoke my privileges here."

Leona's jaw dropped. "What? Are you serious?"

Bella sighed. When she got like this, that little voice in her head started playing on loop, reminding her of every time she had failed in the past and how she would always be behind and be a screw-up, just like her peers used to tell her. Then that self-doubt would make her say things she would later regret.

"You just think that I'm some little girl playing nurse or something. You have no confidence that I can do this job. I want to prove you wrong, but with you knocking me down every chance you get, I don't see how I could."

Leona shook her head. "I know you're more mature than this, Bella. What's going on?"

"Are you telling me I'm wrong?" Bella asked.

"Bella, I am your biggest cheerleader here. I want you to succeed." Leona hesitated, then continued. "I didn't want to tell you this, but yesterday, when you were tired, you missed some steps with patients. I'm only telling you this now to prove to you that I'm on your side. It happens, and I covered for you because I want you to succeed. You are a passionate and gifted worker when it comes to communicating with patients. You can do anything you set your mind to. I know this. And I do think you're going to make a wonderful nurse. But you have to practice better self-care and know your limits."

Bella winced. "I *was* tired, but you shouldn't have covered for me. I don't want you to feel like you have to do that."

Leona moved closer. "I help people out when they matter to me. And you matter to me. Why can't you see that?"

Bella's breath caught, all the fight leaving her body. "I matter to you?"

"Yes. A lot. Why can't you see that?" Leona repeated. She moved closer, so close Bella could feel her breath on her cheek. "But you've raised concerns about feeling like I'm your boss and I don't want to cross any lines. I don't want you to feel pressured or like you have to—"

Bella grabbed the sleeves of Leona's lab coat and pulled their bodies together. She kissed Leona with a passion that surprised her, feeling half out of her mind for doing something like this. Being this bold wasn't like her at all. She had plans that she wanted to stick to, and Leona wasn't part of that. But she couldn't hold back any longer. So much uncertainty and confusion about her life was eating away at her insides and she needed the comfort of Leona's arms.

To her relief, Leona kissed back, resting her hands on the sides of Bella's waist. Bella's knees went weak, and she nearly collapsed. Her head was spinning. The world faded as Bella closed her eyes and just let the kiss sweep them both away. But she wasn't content with just standing there and letting the kiss continue to deepen. She wanted to wrap her fingers through Leona's hair and embrace her with a hunger that continued to leave her knees shaking.

She slowly lifted her hand to Leona's chest, Leona's heart racing beneath her fingers. "Leona," Bella gasped, slowly pressing her back.

"I know," Leona said. Her cheeks were flushed but her eyes were soft. "You have a boyfriend. We shouldn't."

Bella fell backward. She had completely forgotten about Jackson. She certainly hadn't been thinking about him while she has been passionately kissing Leona. What kind of girlfriend was she? She shook her head, her heart shifting as she stared into the eyes of the woman she just wanted to throw her arms around.

"That wasn't what I was going to say," Bella whispered.

"What were you going to say?" Leona's eyes lit up. There was a sweet, sexy grin on her lips.

Bella opened her mouth but was unable to get the words out because Leona's phone decided to ring. In one swift second, the moment was gone. Leona's eyes darkened as she read the message.

"I'm needed in the ER. There's a pediatric trauma patient coming. Can we finish this talk later?"

Bella nodded and watched as Leona rushed from the room, the memories of the kiss unable to fade from her mind. She needed to let Leona know that Jackson wasn't someone who could turn her away from Leona. Still, she would need to tell Jackson the truth. Her heart grew heavy with that burden, but there was no other way around that.

CHAPTER ELEVEN

Leona

The elevator dinged and Leona slowly got off, entering the pediatric floor. It'd been a long night, and she still had two hours to go. How was she going to make it? She had tried so hard to save her last patient but...She felt a tear escape from her eye and closed her eyes.

Be strong, Leona. You still have a job to do. She wiped away the tear and opened her eyes. If she kept telling herself that, maybe she would eventually believe it.

As she rounded the corner, she spotted Bella. Bella rushed up to her, and Leona wanted Bella to just hold her, but they were in the middle of the ward, and that would have raised too many questions. Instead, she simply nodded.

"I was wondering if you would ever come back up here," Bella said, her voice lighthearted and airy.

"What are you still doing here?" Leona asked, barely making eye contact. "I thought you were off at three."

"I was, but Dr. Whalen needed help with a breathing treatment on a patient, Joey. He couldn't get to sleep and started having an asthma attack. It was sort of last minute. I didn't mind staying, though. I'll get home in plenty of time to get three hours of sleep before I head to school."

Leona gave a weak smile, knowing this was a sore subject for Bella. "Remember, just don't push yourself too hard."

"I won't," Bella replied. "How was your trauma patient?"

Leona looked to Bella, and she couldn't stop the tears from falling. Bella's eyes grew wide, and she grabbed Leona's hand and pulled her toward the room they had embraced in. The place they had passionately made out in was now a place Leona would crumble in front of Bella.

"What happened?" Bella asked.

When Leona looked up and met Bella's concerned stare, Bella pulled her into her arms and hugged her. There was a warmth in that hug that left Leona feeling safe and secure, despite the heartache that was crushing her chest.

"I lost her," she said. "Only two years old and I couldn't save her. Maybe I'm not the doctor I thought I was."

Bella pulled back from the embrace and met Leona's eyes. She shook her head. "I'm sure you did everything you could to save that little girl. What happened is not your fault."

"But—" Leona started to argue.

Bella brushed her hand against Leona's cheek and Leona closed her eyes, moving into that very touch. Why was she feeling all these things that were wrong in so many ways? She knew Bella wasn't available and she should have backed off from her deep desires. Instead, she clung to them like they brought her life. It was wrong, and now she was paying the price for that. She was destined to have another heart broken—hers.

"You were *not* the problem, Leona. I wasn't there, but I know that in my heart."

Leona swallowed the lump in her throat and nodded. It was harder to believe than that, though. She was the one sent there to assist in taking care of the little girl. But the trauma was too much. The girl had fallen into a pond and had been without air for too long. By the time she had gotten to the hospital and was rushed into surgery, she was gone. Her brain had been unable to handle the blunt trauma.

Leona wiped a tear away from her eyes and nodded, wanting to hold on to Bella's words. "You shouldn't have to take care of me," Leona argued. "You only have a few hours to rest up."

Bella shook her head. "I'm not worried about that." She once again reached up and stroked her warm hand against Leona's cheek. Leona thought she saw passion behind that stare of Bella's. It felt nice. She also remembered Bella's hand on her chest, pushing her away from their earlier kiss. No matter how much she wanted to kiss Bella again, she resisted. She didn't know what Bella wanted or what any of this meant for them.

Bella didn't initiate anything, either. They only stood there in an embrace, gazing into each other's eyes as Bella touched Leona's cheek. As Bella parted her lips to say something, a voice came from behind them.

"Oh…Pardon me."

Leona pulled away and turned to see Stella, one of the late-night housekeepers, standing there. She had a wide-eyed stare and her jaw was hanging open. "I'll come back," she stuttered.

"No need," Leona said. "We were just leaving."

As they left, Leona had a slight smirk on her lips, despite the pain she felt in her heart. She could only imagine what thoughts were roaming through Stella's head over finding Bella and Leona in that intimate embrace on the hospital grounds. Once out in the hallway, she turned to Bella. "I hope that wasn't too awkward for you."

"Surprisingly, no," Bella said. There was even a grin on her lips. She then frowned. "I'm so sorry about your patient, though. I know that must not be an easy thing to go through."

Leona shook her head and started to open her mouth when she spotted Dr. Crowley headed her way. Leona looked down at her watch. "You're early," she said. Heather Crowley was the doctor set to take her place when she was off the clock. She still had well over an hour and a half to go.

"I heard the news," she said. "Thought maybe you'd want to head out early."

Leona nodded, sighing with relief. "I appreciate that." One thing that caused her anxiety was having to finish her shift after losing a patient. "Thank you."

Heather nodded. "Happy to help, and I'm sorry about your loss."

Bella and Leona went to the elevator and took it to the main floor to get their items from their lockers. As they were leaving the breakroom, Bella turned to Leona. "I don't think you should go home alone. Come with me."

Leona frowned. "You need your rest."

"Sleep is overrated and right now what matters is being with you."

Leona smiled and followed as Bella led the way to the stairwell. Leona didn't inquire as to where they were going as they walked up one set of stairs after another. Finally, Bella opened a door, and they stepped outside to the roof. The whole sky was lit up with stars.

"Wow," Leona gasped.

"Found this place by accident when I came to the hospital for my interview. Isn't this amazing? Rumor has it that just over that horizon you can watch the sun rise. Some say it's the most magical thing you'll ever witness."

Leona nodded, her eyes cast over to where Bella pointed. Silence hit them as they looked far off into the distance. It would be a while before the sun would rise, and Leona didn't want to hope that they would still be out there. After all, Bella did have classes to attend and couldn't possibly waste her morning with her.

"Wanna talk about it?" Bella asked gently.

Leona sighed and slowly turned her eyes toward Bella. "Losing a patient is never easy. When I worked in New York, I was with geriatric patients for a big part of my career. The last two years, I moved into pediatrics. I've lost a few kids—ten, to be exact. It never gets easier."

"I can't imagine losing a child. It's heartbreaking, and not just for the parents."

Leona nodded, swallowing the lump that had come back to her throat.

"I'll pray for the family and for you," Bella said softly.

Leona smiled. "Thank you."

She turned and looked back to the spot that Bella had pointed out to her, feeling Bella's eyes on her the whole time. "It's one of the reasons I asked you to simply entertain the possibility of another career." She turned and met Bella's eyes and she continued. "I've been doing this job for a while, and I love it. I wouldn't want to do anything else but be a doctor. But that's me, and not everyone feels that way. You're young and I wanted to save you the heartache. There are days even worse than this when it feels like the whole world is falling apart. It's hard watching other people go through so much pain and suffering, especially children."

Bella nodded. "I get that. And I appreciate you trying to keep me from having to experience this, but you see, I'm not as weak as I look. I can handle it—the heartache, the sadness, and everything in between. I'm in it for the long haul, wherever the job wants to take me. And I'm sorry for how I reacted earlier. I'm not mad at you. You've made me rethink a lot of things in my life and it's been difficult. I'm struggling with changing my whole idea of the future and I don't know where to go from here."

"I can see that," Leona said. "And I don't think you're weak." Leona reached up and brushed a strand of hair behind Bella's ear. "I don't want to complicate your life, Bella."

"You're not. You won't." Bella shook her head.

"You have a boyfriend," she said.

Bella nodded. "For now," she said. "I know in my heart that I need to end things with him. What you said is true. I've been settling because I've been stuck on this one vision for my life. He's a good man, but my desires have changed. I never expected to meet you."

Bella pulled back a little, hesitating.

"What is it?"

"Will this get us in trouble? Is what we're doing inappropriate? Plus, I don't even know what you want, and—"

Before Bella could fall into a spiral of anxiety and worry, Leona pressed her lips against hers. There were a lot of questions that needed answers and the two of them had a lot to sort through and figure out. But in that moment, none of that mattered. What mattered was that they were in this moment together, alive, safe, with so many possibilities in front of them. Maybe everything around them would crash and burn, but right now, their kiss was the only thing that existed.

———

I CAN'T BELIEVE WE STAYED OUT HERE AND WATCHED THE SUNRISE, Leona thought as she headed into the hospital later that afternoon.

But she had to admit that watching the sunrise with Bella was the highlight of the past four months. If she was being completely honest, it was the highlight of her past year. There was something so raw and real about their conversations together and she couldn't turn from them. Bella had been there in her hour of need and that meant more than anything.

She didn't want the morning to end there, but Bella had to rush off to school. Leona only worried that Bella would fall asleep at the wheel, as Bella had little sleep to go on and five hours of classes that was sure to exhaust her even more.

Leona couldn't stop worrying and sent a text to check in on Bella.

Just checking in with you to make sure you haven't slept through all your classes. I needed this morning. Thank you for being there.

Moments later, Leona's phone vibrated with a response. *I needed it just as much and surprisingly I'm doing pretty well. I don't work tonight, so I'll be sure to get plenty of rest.*

Leona smiled, relieved. *Glad to hear. I'll miss working with you tonight, but please get lots of sleep.*

Bella ended their conversation with a heart-shaped emoji that brought a big smile to Leona's face. There was a sweetness about Bella, which Leona needed in her life, though she knew they both needed to sit down soon and talk about everything and what they each wanted.

Leona's mind stayed steadily on Bella the whole time she went to her locker and took the elevator up to her floor. The moment the elevator doors opened, Jacqueline was there to greet her.

"I'm working with you tonight," she said.

Her voice was high-pitched, and Leona sensed the energy coming from her. Leona mustered up a smile.

Jacqueline continued. "They just brought a patient from ICU

to the ward—Brad Carver. He'll only be here a couple days and then he'll be discharged."

"What room?" Leona asked without hesitancy.

"Four-zero-two," Jacqueline responded.

Before Jacqueline could say anything further, Leona was hurrying toward the room. She wanted to see how Brad was doing. She knocked on the door and entered, seeing Kandice and Brad.

"Leona!" Kandice exclaimed.

"Hi, Lona," Brad said, grinning as he saw her.

"I heard my favorite patient had been moved from the ICU and wanted to see firsthand how he was doing." Leona moved over to the edge of his bed and laid her hand against his forehead. Aside from some yellow bruises and the fact that his arm was in a cast, she could barely tell he had been involved in an accident. And the grin on his face was always a pleasant sight to see.

"I'm doing great!" he said. His infectious grin brought a smile to Leona.

"I'm so glad to hear and see that." She knelt at his level. "Do you need anything? Blanket? Something for pain? A book? Anything?"

Kandice's phone rang, and the social worker stood up. "I have to grab this." She left the room and Leona turned her attention back to Brad.

"Anything at all that will make you more comfortable. You name it."

"A juice box? If it wouldn't be too much trouble. And maybe a pillow to rest my arm."

"At your service. I'll be right back."

She left his room just as Kandice was hanging up. Kandice turned, and Leona saw something in the woman's eyes that alarmed her.

"Just grabbing Brad a pillow and juice box. Everything all right?"

She shook her head. There was a sparkle of a tear in her eyes. "I promised that little boy a home to go to when he leaves here. He expected that and now I'm going to have to break his heart. Which breaks my heart."

Leona frowned. "I don't understand. I thought there was a couple that was excited to bring him to their home. What happened?"

Kandice shrugged despondently. "They seemed so perfect. I thought our little guy would have a shot at real happiness. Looks can be deceiving, though. The guy, turns out, has a previous record. They did the background check, and he didn't pass. Guess it was a minor offense, but the law is that if they have a failed background check, they aren't eligible for the program."

She heaved a sigh. "I should have been more cautious. When things are too perfect, something is bound to happen and screw it all up. There goes that opportunity. And here goes me telling a five-year-old that once he leaves here he'll be going back to a children's home."

Kandice shook her head. "This part of the job sucks. All I ever want to do is help children, not see the pain in their eyes when things like this happen." She turned and went back into Brad's room.

Leona stared at the door, Kandice's words resonating with her. It was all the same, from seeing kids going through pain at the hospital to not surviving their diseases or injuries. But in the end, she did it, because that's what she knew how to do. That's what she loved, even when things didn't always work out in the child's favor.

She grabbed the juice box and pillow and headed back to Brad's room.

"Do you want me to do that?" Jacqueline ran up to her, reaching out for the items in Leona's hands.

"That's all right. I got it," Leona replied.

Jacqueline frowned. "But…you're the doctor…"

"Don't worry Jacqueline; I've got it," Leona reassured her.

She entered Brad's room, aware that Jacqueline was still confused by the fact that Leona was doing something so trivial. Maybe she would understand Leona's ways in due time, but at the same time, she really didn't need to because Bella was Leona's nurse of choice.

"Here you go." She handed Brad the juice and tucked the pillow under his arm. "Better?"

"Much! Thank you!"

She smiled and looked over at Kandice. "Hey, can I talk to you for a minute?"

"Sure." Kandice got up from her chair and followed Leona into the hallway. "Is there a problem? Not with Brad's labs, I hope." Her eyes were wide, and Leona was quick to assure her.

"No. Nothing to do with labs at all." She slipped her hands into her pockets and looked over to his room. "Have you talked to him yet? Tell him that the couple fell through?"

Kandice sighed. "I figured I would give him one restful night. No need in telling him this news when he's just glad to be out of ICU."

"Maybe you don't have to tell him," Leona said, turning back to look at Kandice. Kandice arched an eyebrow, and kept Leona talking. "What if another person came forward to foster him?"

"A person? Or a couple?" Kandice asked.

"I believe that it shouldn't have to be a couple. If someone loves the little guy, isn't that what really matters? Can't a single man or woman come forward and foster?"

"There are no rules against it," Kandice replied. "But who is this person? You?"

Leona nodded. "I don't want to see Brad put in another rough situation. I can take care of him with all the love he could need."

As she spoke, Leona felt her heart swelling. If she didn't do this and Brad ended up getting into another dangerous situation, she'd never forgive herself. That was a fact.

CHAPTER TWELVE

Bella

W
hen Bella got to the hospital the next day, she heard the news that Brad was in one of the rooms and ready to be discharged in a couple of days. She was surprised that Leona hadn't texted her and told her, or, even better, called her. But then again, with the way they had left things, she wondered if maybe Leona was regretting their night together.

She had two objectives once she got to work: Find Leona and gauge where her thoughts were and check on Brad. Stepping off the elevator she looked around for Leona but couldn't find her. Disappointed, she headed straight for Brad's room and knocked.

"It's open," he called out. She entered the room and saw he was alone. "Hey, Bella." He met her with his cheery grin.

What a sight to see, Bella thought happily. "Hey, bud. How's it going?"

"Good!"

"I'm so glad to see your smiling face. Is everyone treating you well?"

"Yep! Lots of loving."

She grinned. "I'm glad to hear that. I went to your old room, and they told me you were here. Super stoked to hear that. And I hear you'll be leaving us in a couple of days. I bet you're looking forward to getting out of here."

"I like the people here," he said. "But yeah, I won't miss this place."

Bella laughed. "I don't blame you. But the food isn't so bad, right?"

He shrugged. "Chicken nuggets are good. And French fries. I also love the juice boxes." He held up one. "This is my third."

"Then you probably have to go to the restroom."

He giggled. "Just got back to the bed."

"All right then. You should be good for a few minutes at least." She ruffled up his hair with her hands. "I have to get to work, but you know how the button works. Let me know if you need anything."

"I will." He took a sip of his juice.

Bella looked over to the empty chair. "Where's Kandice? Has she been here?"

He shrugged. "She's in a meeting or something. I'm fine, though."

"All right, hon. I'll just be right outside your door. Holler if you need anything."

Bella left his room and went to the nurses' station. She grabbed the folder that listed everyone's schedule and flipped it open, scanning her eyes over the schedule. Her jaw dropped when she saw the schedule had been flipped and Jacqueline was scheduled with Leona, leaving her with Dr. Whalen. It was worse than Bella thought. Leona must've really wanted to make sure they wouldn't grow any closer. Her gut tightened, and she closed the folder and sighed out of frustration as she walked out to start her shift.

"Hey, Bella!"

She turned, spotting a smiling Tori at the desk. "Hey. I noticed I'm with Dr. Whalen today. I thought..." Her words trailed off, and she shrugged. "Guess it doesn't matter."

"Oh. You're wondering why you're not with Dr. Guillano?" Bella simply nodded. "She had some things she needed to do today and wouldn't be able to be in until later. They switched, that's all. I'm sure next week you'll be back to being on her schedule."

Tori turned and left to attend to someone, but Bella frowned at the explanation. She wasn't as confident that it was just that simple. What if Leona was afraid that Bella would continue to pursue her and didn't want that? That would complicate them working together, so she almost understood why Leona would change the schedules.

Yet, deep down, she wanted to believe that it was only because Leona had some engagements she couldn't get out of. That would explain everything. Even though that nagging suspicion still dance around inside her mind. All she could do was go about her day and hope that her thoughts would drift from Leona.

It didn't work. At every turn, she caught herself thinking about all the reasons Leona might have pushed Bella off her rotation, and none of them were positive. When Leona came in at the end of Bella's shift, Bella was prepared to tell her that she was sorry and didn't mean to cause any discomfort in their relationship.

Leona walked up and approached her like nothing was wrong, which only confused Bella further. "Wasn't that awesome that Brad was moved out of ICU?" she asked with a wide grin that halted Bella's fears.

"Uh, yeah. Great. I'm a little surprised that you didn't call to tell me. Even a text would have sufficed. You know how much he means to me."

Leona's face fell. "I'm sorry. I guess I wanted it to be a surprise. We were busy last night and it just slipped my mind to let you know. I knew you were going to be here today, though."

Bella nodded. "Would have been nice to have the heads up and all. That's all."

Leona frowned. "I apologize. I should have told you."

Bella released a breath. "It's all right. I was just surprised. That's all." She turned from her. "But I hope you have a good night."

Leona reached out and surprised Bella by grabbing her arm. "You seem upset with me," she said.

Bella looked over her shoulder to see a concerned expression written all over Leona's face. "Just tired, and I guess my thoughts got carried away. I was surprised you weren't working with me. And if I'm being honest, I guess a little disappointed, too. I thought maybe it was because…" Her voice dropped. "Never mind."

"I had some meetings, but I'm sorry. I should have told you. It had nothing to do with what happened between us. Nothing." She had a small smile that helped ease Bella's anxiety. "But I do have some things to discuss with you. Maybe we can have dinner or something this weekend."

"Yeah, sure. We'll compare our schedules. Have a good night." With that, Bella left her. She felt a little rattled by guilt because she sounded like she was still upset, but she did believe everything would be all right between them. As long as she was open to listen to whatever it was Leona wanted to say.

CHAPTER THIRTEEN

Leona

It was a quiet night as Leona worked her rooms and dictated a few orders to Jacqueline, leaving the young nursing assistant to focus much of her time stocking rooms and sterilizing instruments. Leona walked off the elevator from her break at midnight and spotted Jacqueline at the nurses' station. She looked up when Leona approached her.

"I was just about to make my midnight rounds for meds. Will you look and verify these before I go around?"

"Sure."

Leona sat down in front of the computer and looked through the patients and their prescribed medicines. When she got to room four-one-two, she frowned. "Isn't Malcolm allergic to penicillin?"

"Um, I don't know." Jacqueline sat down at the other computer, typed in her credentials, and skimmed through the medical records. She nodded. "Yeah, at eight he had a severe allergic reaction. Nearly died."

Leona shook her head. "Jacqueline, we can't make these kinds of mistakes. If I would have missed that and approved these orders, you would have given it to him, and he could have died." She shook her head. "We're going to have to note this error to the hospital's safety team."

Jacqueline frowned. "But I didn't," she argued. "Most of those meds were put in before I even got here tonight. It wasn't me." Leona saw tears spring to Jacqueline's eyes.

Leona turned back to the orders and scrolled down until she spotted Bella's name. Her eyes darkened, and she knew there was only one person to blame over this matter. Maybe Bella had been too tired or distracted. Either way, she had missed the order, which could have resulted in grave consequences.

"It was me," Leona said.

"Excuse me?" Jacqueline asked.

Leona turned to her. "I had just gotten here. I've been distracted because I lost a patient a couple days ago. I rattled off drugs and I distinctly remember telling Bella to put Malcolm down for penicillin to fight his infection. It was all my fault."

Jacqueline's eyes narrowed and she nodded.

Leona turned back to the computer and made a few changes before signing off on the meds. "You're good to go." She got up from the computer and hurried away.

She was going to have to talk to Bella about this mistake, but how? She didn't want to come across as accusatory, even if Bella needed to understand her mistake could have had dire consequences. At least she had caught it, but she shuddered at the thought that she could have faced another child's death, only this time at the hands of one of the nurses, and over something that could have been avoided.

Even though she tried to not think about it until she could actually have a conversation with Bella, the thought of what could have happened wouldn't stop plaguing Leona's mind. Errors happened all the time, but those types of errors that you could avoid changed the game. Leona couldn't just keep it to herself when it was something that could have significant implications.

When seven o'clock rolled around, Leona wasn't just physically exhausted, but emotionally exhausted, too. She yawned, heading to the elevator to go downstairs, grab her things, and leave for the day. She was looking forward to getting home and trying to put the night behind her. She spotted Tori heading to the desk, the staff schedule folder in hand.

"Next week's staffing schedules?" Leona asked.

"Yep. Hot off the press." She laughed, then tilted her head. "You look like you've been run over by a truck, then walked a million miles. Rough night?"

Leona reached up and touched her hair. It was a mess, she was sure of it. Not to mention the dark circles under her eyes. Before she went home, maybe she needed to stop somewhere for a massage.

"Yeah, you could say that." She dropped her hand from her hair. "Ready to get home to a glass of wine. Or a massage; that would be nice."

"Before eight o'clock?" Tori's eyes widened.

"Tells you the kind of night I had." Leona let out a breath and grabbed the book from her. "But I'll probably wait at least until two. Don't want to cause too much hysteria. Have a good day, Tori."

"You too, Dr. Guillano."

Leona looked down at her own schedule and was glad to see Bella was back on it. For one, she could have an easier time meeting up with her, and for another, she could ensure that Bella knew her mistake wasn't going to change how Leona felt about her.

They would both just learn from it. She closed the folder and put it back, then headed to the elevator.

When the doors opened, Brian Chandler, the CEO, stood there. "Good morning," Leona said. She glanced at her watch. "You're here early." Not to mention out of his own plush office, which she hadn't seen often since starting her job at Capmed.

He nodded firmly. "Had a few things to take care of this morning. Do you mind sticking around a bit so we can talk?"

She frowned and shook her head. "Not at all."

"Let's go to my office."

That elevator ride was slow and painfully awkward. He didn't speak to her, and she was too confused as to why he was even there that she didn't know what to say to him. But finally, they did reach the floor, and he led the way to his office. Leona couldn't help but notice that a few of the employees coming in for their shifts looked over to her like she was walking to the guillotine. But why? Did they know something she didn't?

They entered a room, where three other men, none of whom she knew, were already sitting. She glanced between everyone, even more confused by the turn of events.

"Am I in trouble?" she asked.

Brian looked over to her. "Have a seat. We just need to discuss something with you."

Leona sank into a chair, feeling like a little kid getting ready to be scolded. Leona scanned her eyes between the four men, waiting for one of them to go first. Her hands started to sweat, and she feared she'd hyperventilate if they didn't start soon.

In all her years of being a doctor, she'd never feared she would be reprimanded at her job. Then again, Capmed was a whole new realm for her. She just hoped she didn't start crying when they gave her the metaphorical slap on the hand over whatever it was they were there to discuss with her.

"It has been brought to our attention," Brian started, meeting Leona's gaze, "that you entered an order for penicillin to a pediatric patient that happens to be allergic to penicillin."

Leona gawked at him. "And it was resolved before the error was carried through."

He nodded. "So we were told, but it doesn't change the fact that an adverse event nearly happened and that kid could have been deathly ill as a result. At Capmed we don't tolerate those types of errors. If we get word of it, then we are required to take remedial action."

Leona's mouth snapped closed. "By action…meaning, what?"

"It will go on your record as a point. Once you hit three points, then we'll be forced to seek termination." He shifted a pile of papers and then slid one paper in front of her. "You will be required to sign this, stating you understand that you've been spoken to and will be more careful next time."

Leona released a heavy sigh. Unfortunately, it came out as a haughty laugh. "This isn't a laughing matter," one of the men said.

"I'm sorry. I wasn't laughing, and believe me, after I caught the error, I couldn't think much about anything else. I know how serious this matter is and can assure you I wouldn't laugh over this." She took in a breath. "I lost a patient a few days ago. Losing a patient is never easy, but I would say it distracted me a bit. I usually am on top of things, and it pains me to think about what could have happened."

She looked down at the paper and pen before her. It was a simple form, just describing the policy of Capmed and then one line for her signature and date. She looked back up, this time turning to Brian. "So, Jacqueline told you, right?"

He returned her stare. "We can't disclose the whistleblower in this situation, and I believe you understand that."

She nodded but knew that was the only logical explanation.

Had Jacqueline wanted to get Leona in trouble to ease the stress of the mistakes she had made herself? She couldn't blame her if that were the case, but it was a messed up situation. She looked back down at the paper and grabbed the pen. She wouldn't fight it because it beat the alternative of Bella getting raked over the coals. Leona could get out of this situation, but she was an established doctor. Bella was just a nursing assistant. Perhaps that was another reason Jacqueline wanted Leona to get in trouble over the matter.

"It won't happen again," Leona said, pushing the paper toward Brian.

"We have all heard amazing thing about your performance so we're confident it won't. Thank you."

She nodded. "Am I free to go?"

He nodded and all the men got up from the table and watched her as she left the room. She wasn't sure why the other men had to be there, unless they needed some sort of board to acknowledge that she did, in fact, sign the form. But it was over and done with, and she would have to try to forget that it happened. She went and grabbed her purse from her locker, then left the hospital.

As she got to her car, she sat in the driver's seat for a moment, pulling her phone from her pocket to text Bella. The sooner they got together, the better she would feel about everything she had to tell her. Before she could start the text message, her phone rang.

"This is Leona," she started.

"Hello, Leona. It's Kandice. I was hoping you had some time this morning for us to could sit down and chat."

Leona stifled a yawn, feeling the heavy weight from all that transpired, but she needed to take this meeting. Then she would know exactly how she could proceed.

CHAPTER FOURTEEN

Bella

Bella looked up from her anatomy book and stared straight ahead. It was only two, but she was already dressed for her seven o'clock work shift. Still, she thought of a million reasons she should call out. She could tell them she was sick. Surely they wouldn't want someone that was running a fever to come in and work.

But then you'd be lying.

She hadn't seen Leona since they had passed one another during the shift change, and she had definitely felt an awkwardness between them. If they couldn't even acknowledge their intimate encounters, what did that say for them?

Before she could make the call, her phone rang, and she saw Jackson's name. "Hey, Jackson." Her head started pounding, and she massaged her temples.

She'd been avoiding him, but there were only so many times she could ignore his calls before facing the facts. She wanted to talk to him in person, but everything was starting to wear her down too much. She didn't know where her life was headed or where she stood with Leona, but she knew she needed time to breath and figure out her life without Jackson in the back of her mind. Her stomach churned as she considered what she was about to say.

"Hey, babe." Bella could practically see Jackson beaming on the other end of the line. "Just was thinking about you. Are you free tonight so that we can meet up for dinner or something? I've missed you."

If she called in sick, she could meet with him and have the conversation she needed to have with him. Then again, she would have an absence on her record. She needed to get this out now. Then they could have a longer talk in the future.

The words came out of her, raw and blunt. "Jackson, I need a break."

"Uh, from school or work? If you want to take a weekend trip somewhere—"

"No. I want us to take a break. I'm sorry I can't tell you this in person. Everything is...I'm so overwhelmed and I need some time to think about everything. I don't know how I feel about us anymore and I feel awful about it, but this isn't fair to you. We need to take a break from our relationship so we can both think about what future we want."

Jackson was silent for so long, Bella worried the call had dropped. Finally, he said, "I don't understand. What changed? The plan was always to get married and have kids. I still want that. You don't?"

"I don't know what I want, but right now I need time, so can we put a pause on us?"

"Can we at least talk about this in person?"

"I wish I could, but I have to work and...I'm sorry."

"I'm sorry, too."

She felt a pang of regret for letting him down, but she couldn't keep stringing him on like this. "I want to talk in person. I just don't know when. I'm sorry, I have to go."

"I love you."

"Bye."

She ended the call and wiped tears from her cheek. Had she done the right thing? Jackson had been with her so many years, and she didn't even know what Leona wanted. Maybe asking Jackson to go on a break was wrong, but a weight had lifted from her that she hadn't realized she was carrying.

A text message came through and she looked down to read who it was from.

Leona: I need to see you. Can you come over in two hours to my house?

Bella: Text me your address.

After already having one difficult conversation today, why not go for two and get it over with? At least she'd know where Leona stood one way or another.

Bella wondered if she should dress in normal clothes, but that would look strange, especially when she wasn't sure how long she'd be there. She decided to stay in her scrubs and headed over to Leona's house an hour and a half later.

Leona lived in a subdivision thirty minutes from Bella's apartment. When Bella pulled up in front of her house, her jaw dropped. It was much more lavish than the apartment Bella lived in. Not that she would have expected anything less from a successful doctor like Leona.

When Leona opened the door, Bella started taking off her shoes, but Leona just laughed. "That's not necessary."

Bella moved into the foyer and gawked at the furnishings surrounding her. "You have a nice place here," she commented.

"Thanks. I was lucky. I saw it on the market two weeks before I was to start the job. Placed an offer sight unseen. I was the first one. They accepted the offer and I just hoped that I wouldn't regret it. I have to say that it could have turned into my biggest regret."

"But some things actually work out," Bella concluded.

"Yep, and this is one of those things." Leona looked around her home and then glanced back at Bella. "How are you doing?"

"Doing fairly well. Got plenty of sleep over the past day and a half, so that's promising. School has been busy, but when is it not?" She slid her hands into the pocket of her scrubs, then shrugged, forcing the words out to see how Leona would react. "And I told my boyfriend I wanted a break."

Leona looked up, her face unreadable. Her lips faded into a straight line, and she motioned toward a hallway. "Would you like some coffee?"

Not the reaction Bella had hoped for. "Sure."

Bella followed Leona down the hallway and to a kitchen, where a pot had already been brewed for them. Leona poured her a cup, then they moved over to a table and sat down. It was after two sips that Leona cleared her throat and looked up.

"I want to start by saying that I know things have been rough on you. You've had a tiring and exhausting schedule. I don't even know how you've been managing. So, when I tell you what I'm about to tell you, know that I'm not here to scold you. I'm not here to make you feel bad about yourself. And in no way do I want you to take this as criticism because I know you've been struggling. This is a learning experience and I know that once we work through this, you *will* able to grow from it. We're a team at work, so I'm telling you this as your teammate who only wants the best for you."

The more Leona spoke about how she didn't want Bella to take offense to whatever it was she was about to say, or how she didn't want to sadden Bella or make her mad, the more uneasy Bella grew. Her muscles tensed. Leona was spewing a lot of words without saying much at all. That meant that Bella had something to worry about.

"You're giving me a complex. Just tell me what's going on. Please."

"Yesterday you left the hospital with a penicillin order for one of your patients. They're allergic to penicillin. Please tell me that Dr. Whalen told you to order it."

Bella's jaw dropped. "Who's the patient?"

"Malcolm Little."

Bella looked down at her coffee mug. The flood of memories came rushing back to her, starting with how Dr. Whalen had run through the list of patients she should prescribe meds to. Malcolm had been one of them, but she had specifically recalled reading his allergy for penicillin. Dr. Whalen had ordered erythromycin instead. She must have inadvertently put in the wrong medication when she had transcribed the orders.

Bella fought to explain herself. "I, I guess I was tired. And I had a lot on my mind." She met Leona's gaze, which had significantly darkened. "I was worried that you were regretting that we had gotten close and when I didn't see you on my rotation, I suspected you had changed your shift to avoid me."

She wiped a tear that had escaped from her eyes. "I'm sorry, but what does this mean? Am I dropped from the program? Am I barred from becoming a nurse? Have these last four years been for nothing?" Panic rose inside of her as the questions tumbled out.

"Malcom didn't get the medicine, I hope." She jumped up from the table and started to pace back and forth in front of Leona. "I should apologize to his parents. How could I make such a huge mistake? Maybe I really am not cut out to be a nurse and—"

"Bella, calm down," Leona spoke. "This is precisely what I wanted to prevent. I didn't want you panicking. It's true this was a grave mistake and could have cost Malcom his life. But all is well. I spotted the error and I defused the situation. He got his meds—the right ones —and there's no reason to fret over that. But…" Her words trailed off. Bella stopped pacing and turned to her. "Jacqueline caught the error."

Bella groaned. "So she's one-upped me. Now I'll be the one that they say doesn't deserve to stay on at Capmed when the program ends."

Leona shook her head. "I told her that I gave you the orders to put the penicillin in. She thinks that I'm the one that caused the issue."

"You shouldn't have covered for me like that. I don't want anyone to think negatively of you. And I don't want your pity. If I made a mistake, I'll own up to it and suffer the consequences."

Leona shook her head. "It's too late to worry about that. Jacqueline went to the board and told them about what happened, and they reprimanded me for it. If things change now, they'll wonder why I covered for you. Frankly, that would be a worse situation to be in. We'll just leave it at that.

"I'm fine with the way it went down, but I just wanted to make sure you knew what had happened. And again, I want to stress that you *need* to get your rest. I believe in your abilities as a nurse, but anyone who is so severely sleep deprived, as you've been, will make mistakes. This isn't from a lack of ability. It's from a lack of cognitive function because you're not allowing your body to recover."

Bella's jaw clenched. She was annoyed that Jacqueline would have willingly done something to get Leona into trouble. She was also upset that it was all her fault. She shook her head.

"It's not right. This is on me. I need to do better. I can do better. I can't imagine you taking the blame for it. Let me do something to fix this."

Leona reached across the table as Bella fell back into her seat. "There's nothing you can do now. I am telling you that if you say something, they'll question why I covered for you, and I could be fired. This is the best option. Remember, we're a team, so it's okay that I took the blame for this."

Bella was startled by the tenacity in Leona's eyes, but when she spoke like that, Bella knew she was right. She couldn't watch Leona get fired over her trying to protect her. That would make for an even harder thing to face.

"Did you get yelled at too badly?" Bella asked, looking down to see that Leona's hand was still in hers. Leona didn't pull away, and neither did Bella.

"It wasn't too harsh. I had to sign a letter and got a point in my chart. But I know that it would have been harder to go through if you would have gotten the lashing. They probably would have thrown you from the program."

"And it would've been well deserved," Bella mumbled.

Leona slipped her fingers between Bella's and moved in closer to her. "Don't say that. I'm glad you're at Capmed and I don't want you to get fired over something like this. I know that you'll remember next time to double and triple check your work. It's something we all have to be mindful of. But as far as anyone knows, I'm the one that ordered this drug, and you were only going on my orders. Got that?"

Bella nodded. "But what about Dr. Whalen?"

Leona shrugged. "I thought of that, too. He would know that he was the one who ordered it, but it's against protocol for the hospital to disclose when doctors get reprimanded, especially with their peers. I don't think that Jacqueline will go running her mouth, because frankly, that was poorly done on her side. No one would take it too kindly if they realized Jacqueline was the hospital snitch. That would stay with her."

It made sense, but Bella was still upset that she had messed up and gotten someone else in trouble for it. She didn't want Leona to always have to take the fall for her. Yet, she appreciated that Leona had done so without hesitation.

"I appreciate that you covered for me. I really do. Thank you."

She smiled. "There wasn't even a doubt that I would." She slowly pulled her hand back. "But on that note, that's not the only thing I have to tell you."

Bella groaned. "Should I start cringing already?"

Leona laughed loudly. "I don't think so. I think you'll be surprised, but hopefully pleasantly so. I have to say that I'm a little shell-shocked myself."

Bella tilted her head, anxious to hear what it was. It wasn't long before Leona started excitedly chattering away.

"I'm not sure what you've heard, but Brad's foster family fell through."

Bella's jaw dropped. The thought that Brad wasn't getting his temporary home killed her, but she waited for Leona to continue, hoping she would say something positive.

"The man didn't pass the background check. But that's only half the story, and frankly, it gets better."

Bella sighed. "That's a relief."

"Because there wasn't another family readily available and because Brad is set to go home tomorrow, I inquired about being his foster mom."

Bella jumped up, gawking at Leona. "Are you serious?"

Leona frowned. "That's a good 'are you serious,' right?"

Bella laughed. "The best, but *are* you serious? You would foster him? How would that even work, with you being a doctor with such erratic hours? He would be left home alone a lot."

Leona grinned. "I've covered all the bases. There's a day care at the hospital. When he's at school I can work around their schedule. I want a family, and I think that ideally, I'll foster him with the plan of eventually adopting him."

Bella grinned. This was by far the best news she'd had in a while. "I think this is a fantastic idea," Bella said. "And I think my sister would love to watch him, too, if you're ever too busy." She paused. "But are we getting our hopes up too soon? I mean, you inquired about it, but it doesn't necessarily mean it will go through, right?"

"I got the call yesterday morning. It's official."

Without a second thought, Bella grabbed Leona by the arms and pulled her up, then threw her arms around her and pulled her into an embrace. "I'm so happy for you."

"You can see him whenever you want," Leona whispered. She moved into the embrace, kissing Bella with the same enthusiastic passion Bella had felt their first kiss.

The news was exciting for sure, but the way she felt in Leona's arms was even more so, and Bella wanted to be nowhere else. All of the unknowns between them, though, made her break the kiss.

"Wait," Bella said. "I just need to know where we stand. I've spent the past few days lost and confused. And I can't promise anything. I don't even know what I want right now, but...I do know that I like you."

Leona smiled. "I like you, too." She stepped away, the brief moment of joy on her face replaced by seriousness. "Things are complicated, aren't they?"

"Yeah. I told my boyfriend we need a break, but I haven't decided what future I want. It's been hard enough just getting through school. And I know it's not fair to you to string you along. Even if I want for us to...Well, I don't know if my heart..."

Leona took Bella's hand. "I understand. Honestly, I'm a little hesitant, too. My focus needs to be on Brad for now. But I still want to spend time with you."

"Even if we don't know what the heck we're doing?"

Leona smiled. "Especially that."

They kissed, a soft kiss that made Bella feel like everything would work out, even if she had no idea it would.

———

BELLA ENTERED BRAD'S ROOM TO SEE LEONA LOOKING OVER the guy, who was still sound asleep. Leona looked like the doting mother Bella knew she would be. Leona turned to Bella, grinning, and Bella motioned for her to follow her into the hall.

"I have to go because I have class, so I won't be here when you get to take him home. But is he super stoked?"

Leona grinned. "Extremely. I think he can't believe that he's leaving the hospital and going to a loving home. I can't wait until he sees his bedroom. We're going to decorate the spare room together. I'm going to make sure he feels that he's loved every day he's there with me."

"He's one lucky boy," Bella replied. "I called Veronica on break and told her I might have a babysitting gig for her. She can do it when she's not at school. She's really excited. I told her that it was a doctor I work with."

Leona's eyes fell, and Bella reached out to touch her arm. "I haven't told my family yet about Jackson."

She looked up and nodded. "I get it."

Bella sighed with relief. "Well, I'd better go, but I'll call you later. I hope things go smoothly when you get him home."

"I'm sure they will. Thanks, Bella." Leona looked past her, her eyes darting around the hospital.

Bella glanced over her shoulder. The hospital was empty of

people. Leona grabbed her hand and pulled her back into Brad's room and closed the door. Then, she moved in and captured a kiss without having to worry about being watched by anyone, including the hospital cameras.

"I'll talk to you soon," Bella said, pulling from the kiss.

As Leona turned back to her foster son, Bella left the room and went downstairs to get her purse and leave the hospital to get to her class. She yawned several times on the way to the hospital, suddenly laden with how tired she truly was. It was going to be a long four hours, but she would have to somehow muddle through them.

At least she was on time. She took her seat before her professor came in and took his place at the front of the class. "Today we are continuing where we left off the last class, finishing our study on the cranium. Turn to page one-oh-two. I want you to study this diagram in its entirety, as we will have a quiz on it next period."

Bella stared at the picture and started to zone out, only vaguely registering the professor's words. Before she knew it, her eyes drifted shut, and she withered into a relaxing sleep.

"Ms. Strong? Ms. Strong, are you paying attention? Answer me, Ms. Strong."

Bella jerked awake when Anthony, the guy in the seat next to her, kicked her foot. "Huh?" she asked, jumping up from her seat. She felt saliva on her lip and quickly wiped the drool away, her classmates laughing all around her.

"I asked you a question. And since I know you were deeply concentrated on it, I look forward to hearing your response."

"Um…" she looked over to Anthony, hopeful he would send her the response telepathically. He smirked and shook his head. She turned back to look at Professor Finch. "The right lower quadrant?" she asked.

"Is that a question?" he asked. Again, students laughed around her, and she shook her head.

"No, it's definitely the right lower quadrant."

Professor Finch looked down at his book, then back up. "Well, if we were discussing the abdomen, then you might be right. Have a seat and see me after class."

Bella sat back down and looked at the book. *The cranium. Ugh. Could I have been any more wrong?*

In a mixed blessing, class went by quickly, but as everyone filtered out of the room, Bella didn't rush to get her things to see what Professor Finch wanted to say to her. She, however, did think of the million things she wanted to say in her apology, but he was a short and curt man who didn't seem to have an empathetic bone in his body, and it wasn't going to suffice him for her to apologize.

"Ms. Strong," he started.

Bella interrupted, "I know what you're going to say and I'm sorry. It's just I've been busy with work and school and I'm not getting much sleep at all. I worked twelve hours and came straight from the hospital. I'm trying here, Professor Finch. You have to believe that."

"Do you know that when I was going to college, I worked sixty hours and did full-time, all the way up to the time I got my doctorate? That's tough work, yet I managed."

Bella dropped her eyes. There was no point in trying to continue her argument. She already knew where it would go. She let him do his own rambling.

"We all have things that keep us busy, but we have to press on if we have any hope to succeed in life. You have to persevere if you want to achieve greater things out of life. A person is their own worst enemy, and if you choose to fail, then you will fail."

"I'm not choosing to fail," she argued.

"Your coursework would beg to differ. Your grades are struggling and if you don't do better, you *will* fail. You have to fight and work even harder if you want to succeed. You can do it, but only if you want it."

"Am I free to go?" She looked away from him.

"Just one more thing. Do you want to achieve bigger and better things out of life? Or do you prefer mediocre?"

"Professor Finch," she stated. "Of course I want that, but maybe I'm not cut out for that. I believe in my heart I'm doing the very best that I can. If that isn't satisfactory then I guess I'll have to live with my failures. But I'm trying."

"If you don't try harder, you might wind up failing this class. Without passing this anatomy course, you won't graduate. Think about that." He handed her a past assignment and she looked at the D written in a boldfaced capital letter. "You say you're better than this? Then prove it."

She yanked the assignment from him and slipped it into her folder. "I'm not a failure and I will show everyone that I can make it through this class." She turned and hurried out of the room.

Bella didn't know how she had gotten a D. She had the book right in front of her when she was going through the assignment. She shook her head and stormed out of the school. She was going to prove everyone wrong. If they didn't think she could do it, then that was on them. Bella was out to make sure she could.

CHAPTER FIFTEEN

Leona

L eona grabbed her phone and flipped through it, checking to see if she had somehow missed Bella's text or phone call. She saw nothing. A day and night had passed and still no contact from her. She knew that Bella had said she would meet with her when classes were through the previous day. Leona had practically been attached to her phone, waiting for a message or call that had never come.

"Lona?" Brad asked, approaching her from behind. She turned to him and lifted him onto her lap.

"What is it, bud?"

He had a serious look on his face, one that melted Leona's heart. She held him closer to her, just thankful to have him there.

"Now that I'm living with you, what should I call you? Should I still call you Lona? Or what?"

She grinned. "Well, what would you like to call me?"

"Mama?" he asked, eyes wide.

Leona grinned, wrapping her arms around him. "I would like that very much, if that's what you feel comfortable with."

He nodded. "Mama Lona."

She laughed, pulling him into her arms. The best two words strung together. "We need to get going so I can get you to the day care."

"Will I be going to school?" he asked. "In the foster homes I was never there long enough, but now…I was just wondering."

"Is that what you want?" He was quick to nod.

Leona smiled, knowing she was going to do whatever she could to make sure Brad grew up happy. Within reason, of course.

"We'll make that happen. But for today, day care."

They got in the car and headed to the hospital. She had plenty of time to get him in the right room and head up to her floor to start her shift. Brad seemed happy and excited to be going to the day care until he reached the room and she was just about to drop him off. He backed up to the wall and just waited. She looked over her shoulder and walked over to him.

"Are you nervous?" she asked.

He nodded, slightly. "What if no one likes me?"

Leona knelt in front of him. "You know, when I first started here, I worried about that, too. I was coming to a new place and thought it would be awkward if I couldn't make any friends. I worried all night about that, but then, when I started, it just felt right, and I've made great friends. Plus, you're a charming young man. I would say you're going to have the kids falling all over you."

He looked up, his grin infectious. "I had a friend, once. Kyle." He looked down at the floor. "Back at my first children's home. Someone adopted him and I haven't seen him in a long time."

Leona nodded. "I understand. It's hard to lose friends that you've made, but I promise you that you're going to make new friends. You have my word on that."

He looked up and his smile grew wider. She grabbed his hand and escorted him into the room. A woman stood with a baby in her arms and another one knelt in front of a little girl as they played with the blocks.

"Who do we have here?" the woman holding the baby asked.

"I'm Dr. Guillano. I work on the pediatric floor. This is Brad. He'll be coming here for a bit, until I can get him signed up for school. I just started fostering him and haven't had a chance to work out a lot of details. I hope this is okay."

"You bet it is," the woman said. "My name is Sheila, and that's Heidi. We work at the day care during the day. How long will we have him today?"

"'Til about midnight," Leona answered.

"Marla does the third shift most nights, so she'll be here when you get here. What time is his bedtime?"

Leona considered that. The previous night he was in bed by seven, but was that his usual bedtime? He had just seemed exhausted, as things had been hectic for him. "Sevenish, I suppose. I won't be one of those parents that have to stick to a regime, so I understand if something happens."

Sheila smiled. "I'm sure we're going to get along just fine. We just need you to sign a waiver that documents the rules, etcetera, but that will be just about it."

"Sounds good. I'm pretty nervous leaving him and all. I just hope he gets along with everyone."

Sheila smiled. "I would say so far, so good." She motioned with her head toward Brad, who was playing with Heidi and the girl with the blocks. A flood of relief washed over her. "How long have you been fostering him?

"About twenty-four hours," Leona mumbled.

Sheila arched an eyebrow and Leona laughed and nodded.

"Wow. That's amazing. I know kids need parents just like you. So, kudos to you."

Leona followed Sheila over to the desk, where the woman fumbled around for some paper, all while keeping the baby jostling in her arms. She sighed and looked down at the baby, then to Leona. "Do you mind?"

"Not at all." Leona grabbed the baby and held the little girl in her arms. She was so small. "How old is she?"

"Twelve weeks. Her mom just went back to work a couple days ago. I send her pictures often, but it's not like the real thing. Here we go." She whipped out a sheet of paper and motioned to where Leona could sign. "I'll fill in the rest of the information for you," Sheila replied. "But you're good to go."

"Thanks a lot." Leona turned to Brad and walked over to where he was playing. She watched him for a minute, then leaned in and kissed the top of his forehead. "I'll see you in a bit."

"Bye, Mama Lona," he said.

She smiled and waved, then looked over to Sheila, then Heidi. "Thank you both."

As she left the room, she felt some guilt. Maybe she shouldn't have left him so soon. He had just been put in her care, and it felt like she was finding reasons to leave him. She turned and looked at him through the door, but he seemed happy and looked like he was enjoying himself. When she turned around, she bumped into a woman who was holding a boy's hand.

"Excuse me," she said.

"No worries." The woman escorted the boy, who looked to be Brad's age, into the room, and Leona felt assured that Brad would find some friends and be just as happy when she picked him up. At least, she hoped that'd be the case. Now all she needed to do was get to work and see Bella. She still questioned why Bella hadn't reached out to her the previous day.

She dropped her purse off at her locker, then headed to her floor and tried looking for Bella. She looked toward the nurse's station, but Bella wasn't there.

Uneasy, Leona went to her office and logged into her computer. She skimmed through the charts to check out the latest things that were happening. She saw that Bella was logged in, so she knew she was at least at the hospital. She got up from her desk to go to her first patient or see Bella—whichever came first.

When she rounded the corner, she finally spotted Bella. That didn't take long. Bella looked up from her notebook and looked straight at Leona. She then turned and darted into the closest room. Leona frowned. Bella was avoiding her. But why? Looking back on their previous encounter, Leona thought nothing would have kept Bella from wanting to see her. Unless something happened after the fact. Or maybe it was because neither of them could commit to being in a relationship or knew how to define whatever it was they had together.

Bella looked like she had been studying while on break, so Leona didn't go after her. Hopefully, they'd get to talk before the day was done.

———

LEONA SLUMPED DOWN IN HER SEAT AND GLANCED AT HER computer. It'd been four hours since they had started their shift and the only times she could get Bella to talk to her were when they concerned patients. She was starting to get a complex, thinking that maybe she had overlooked something she had done wrong.

A knock sounded on the door. She looked up to see Bella.

"Misty needs an approval on meds." She thrust the order out matter-of-factly, and Leona cautiously grabbed it.

"All right." She looked down, surveying the orders, then looked up. "This is something you could have easily approved yourself.

She shrugged. "Don't want to give something I shouldn't have inadvertently."

Leona handed the orders back to her, arching an eyebrow. "I thought we've been through this," Leona began. "I don't want any craziness between us. You made a mistake with your other patient, but it's done, and we have to just move on."

"Fine. Am I free to go?" Bella asked, a look of annoyance streaking across her face. Leona nodded and Bella turned and hurried from the room.

That was odd. Leona had no idea where that came from. Even though they had already talked about it, could Bella actually be upset that Leona had called her out on the medication error?

She sat at her desk, staring at her computer, looking for answers. Answers that weren't there. Her phone started ringing, and she grabbed it. "Dr. Guillano."

"Hey, Dr. Guillano. It's Marla. I'm the third shift director here in the day care."

"Yes, of course. Is everything all right?"

"I'm having a little trouble getting Brad to lie down. If you were here to talk to him, then maybe he would be able to relax. I'm sorry to bother you. I know you're busy and all…"

"No worries. I'll be right there." She dropped the phone into the receiver and jumped up, hurrying out of the office. Bella was sitting at the nurse's station and looked up when she approached. Bella jumped up from her chair, surprised.

"I have to run to the day care," Leona said hurriedly.

"Is everything all right with Brad?" Bella asked, her sour attitude softening.

So she did still remember that Brad was coming to live with her. And yet, she hadn't once inquired about him. They hadn't talked about how Brad factored into any possibility of a relation-ship between them, but maybe Bella's lack of attention meant she wasn't ready for motherhood right now. And Leona couldn't get involved with someone who wasn't going to stick around. It would be too damaging to Brad.

"He can't sleep, so they're asking for my help. Hopefully I won't be long."

Bella opened her mouth to say something, but Leona turned away and left her standing there. She got into the elevator and watched Bella staring after her until the doors closed her in. She collapsed back against the elevator wall, confused.

The day care was quiet when she reached it. The only people there were a woman and Brad. The woman knelt next to Brad, the two of them looking at a book. She looked up when Leona approached them.

She stood and put on a smile. "I'm Marla," she said.

Leona held out her hand. "Dr. Guillano. You can call me Leona."

She immediately knelt in front of Brad. "What's wrong, bud?"

Marla left them alone, and Brad looked at Leona shyly. "It's quiet here."

"The best way to get rest is by having quiet." She rubbed his back, and he looked around the empty room.

"Too quiet," he said.

Leona followed his gaze and then looked back at him. "Too much like a children's home, perhaps?" she asked.

He looked back at her and slowly nodded. Leona sat down on the floor and pulled him onto her lap. "I'm not going to ever send you back there. You know that, right?"

He shrugged and looked down at his hands. She kissed the top of his head, then grabbed the book he had been looking at. She opened it up and began to read it. Before she knew it, he was nestled against her chest, following along. Leona smiled, happy that Brad already seemed so comfortable with her. She continued to read, and twenty minutes later, he was fast asleep. She carefully shifted him so he was resting on a sleeping bag with his head on the pillow.

Leona stood to her feet and looked down at him. He rolled onto his side, turning away from her. She smiled and turned, looking over at Marla. She walked over to her, checking on Brad one more time over her shoulder.

"I'm not sure what you've heard about our situation," Leona began, turning back Marla.

"That he's a foster child," Marla replied. "Really, that's about it."

Leona nodded. "He just came to live with me, and I think his nerves are getting the better of him. He just needs to be reminded that I'll never leave him."

"That makes sense."

Leona looked around the day care. "Will he be the only one here until midnight?" she asked.

"Yeah, I have one child coming in at two." Leona's mouth opened in surprise. "That tends to happen. Babies need to get woken up just to come into the hospital with their mothers or fathers."

"Wow. Well, I'll be back to get him in a few hours."

"No problem. See you then. I'm not going anywhere." Marla smiled and turned to some paperwork on her desk.

Leona watched Brad as she left the day care. She just hoped he didn't wake up, frightened by his surroundings. She couldn't worry about that, though. Not now. She had to get back to work.

When she reached her floor, she didn't see Bella, so she headed straight for her office. It was quiet in there, with Bella the only nurse working the evening shift. Hadley, a cleaning woman, worked also, but that was it. Luckily, it wasn't a busy night.

Leona sat back down at her computer and opened a drawer, where she had stored her water and sandwich in a lunchbox.

She took a bite of her sandwich and leaned back in her chair, releasing a yawn. She closed her eyes. *Nothing a five-minute cat nap couldn't fix.*

When she heard the clearing of a throat, her eyes snapped open.

"I didn't know if you were back," Bella replied, her voice soft.

Leona sat up in her chair and put her sandwich down on her desk. "It didn't take long to get him to go to sleep."

"That's good. I thought I would run and get something to eat. If you think you can handle it, that is."

Leona smirked. "We only have three beds filled. I doubt I'll run into any issues."

Bella started to turn, then looked over her shoulder. "Want anything? Besides that bologna sandwich, I mean."

"No, but thank you."

Bella turned to leave, but Leona couldn't stop herself from speaking. "Are you going to tell me why you're having an attitude with me all of a sudden?"

Bella turned and opened her mouth, but then looked down at the floor. Leona stared at her as Bella started to sob. At first, Leona thought she was misreading the signs, but she saw that Bella's face was bright red and tears were running down her cheeks.

"Bella!" She jumped up and hurried to the door, closing it so they had privacy, even though there wasn't anyone likely to walk in. "What's wrong? And don't tell me this is about the medication error, because I'm not going to buy that."

"It is, and it isn't," Bella mumbled. "I just feel like my life is falling apart. I mess up orders. I'm not doing stellar work at school.

It just seems like everywhere I turn I'm messing up with something." She sniffled and flicked a tear away. "I'm sorry I was snippy with you. I'm exhausted and I don't know how much I can take of this." She slumped her head down and stared at the ground as Leona's heart tugged inside her rapidly beating chest. "And now you probably think I just can't handle things like a normal adult."

"That's not what I'm thinking, Bella." Leona reached up and stroked a strand of hair behind Bella's ear, which had fallen from her ponytail. "Bella, look at me."

Bella shook her head and Leona stroked her hand down the length of Bella's arm. "Please look at me."

After a brief hesitation, Bella looked up, her eyes glazed over from tears. "I'll tell you what I see. When I told you my thoughts that you should remain open to other careers, I barely knew you. But I can tell you that I've changed my thinking on whether you should continue to pursue this. Besides, no one should ever try to talk you out of something you want to do. As for the error, things happen. And as for your classes, I'm sure it's not as bad as you think."

"You have no idea," Bella said.

Leona reached up and brushed her thumb against Bella's cheek, making Bella close her eyes. "I know you. I know that you are a strong, caring, and beautiful individual. And whatever you set your mind out to do, you will achieve it. You just have to believe you're worth achieving it. No one can take that light and that drive from you."

Bella bit down on her lower lip and Leona's eyes dropped to her lips. She moved in and claimed her lips against hers, growing breathless. She slid her tongue along Bella's, then opened her eyes. The heat in Bella's stare ignited a fire between Leona's legs. Leona turned and locked the door, then turned back to Bella. She moved in and kissed her hard, pressing her back until she bumped into her desk.

"I want you, Bella," Leona whispered. "But if you tell me no right now, I'll stop."

Bella's eyes lifted to hers and Bella shook her head slightly before grabbing onto her shirt and pulling it up and over her head, revealing her perfectly round breasts, barely hidden under her bra. With one flick of her wrist, Bella's bra fell to the ground.

Leona moved in, latching her teeth onto one nipple and swirling her tongue around the areola. Bella groaned, and Leona knew she was in the right place, at the right time. Nothing was going to end their heated moment together.

CHAPTER SIXTEEN

Bella

Bella handed a chart over to Jacqueline. "It's all yours. We've been relatively quiet all night. Hope it stays the same."

Jacqueline nodded and yawned. She scowled, then rubbed her face. "Are you exhausted?" she asked. "I feel like no matter how much rest I get, it's just never enough."

Another yawn escaped. This time, Jacqueline groaned, her eyes droopy, and her mouth settled into a thin line. "It's all worth it, right?"

"I'm exhausted, no doubt. I keep telling myself that there's a light at the end of the road. Just need to get through a few more bumps."

Bella looked up and saw Leona moving toward them. Instantly, her mind went to their heated encounter in Leona's office. Things couldn't have gotten sexier than that.

"Have a good morning, Dr. Guillano," Jacqueline spoke up, her voice ringing out loudly.

Leona barely acknowledged Jacqueline as she brushed past her and headed straight to the elevator. When Bella turned back to her, Jacqueline had dropped her gaze to the chart in her hands.

"Anyway, enjoy yourself." Bella tossed a wave, then headed toward the elevator to get on with Leona.

As the elevator doors closed them in, Leona turned and grinned at Bella. "Where were we?" she asked. She pulled Bella to her, catching Bella off guard, but she immediately crashed her lips against Leona's. Leona's tongue slithered into her mouth, making Bella release a moan.

On cue, as the doors opened, they pulled from one another and stepped off onto the main floor. Leona turned to her. "I'm headed this way to get Brad," she said, motioning with her head.

Bella nodded. "So, what was that back there with Jacqueline?"

Leona grimaced. "She's the one who turned me in to the board. Or did I not tell you that?"

Bella winced. "I see." Bella looked past her, then glanced back at Leona. "Guess I'll let you go then."

"Do you have school in the morning?"

Bella shook her head. "Not 'til three o'clock tomorrow."

Leona had a sneaky grin on her lips. She tilted her head at Bella and said, "I'm not sure how you would feel about this, but what would you say about coming back to my place? I could get Brad into bed and then you and I could get into bed." She winked, making Bella smile widely.

The more she considered it, the more she wanted to spend the night with Leona. Just one night of not thinking about her problems or what their future might hold. Was it so wrong to just want some fun, to escape? Eventually, she wouldn't be able to avoid her problems, but for now, she didn't want to think about how everything in her life seemed to be an issue.

"Best idea yet," Bella replied.

Leona nodded, then turned and led the way to the day care. When they got there, the woman working at the desk had her head propped up against her hand and was aimlessly staring at a book. When they opened the door, she looked up, a smile brightening her face.

"Hello, Dr. Guillano," she said.

Leona glanced over at Bella. "This is Marla. She manages the day care during evening hours."

"Hey, Marla, I'm Bella. I'm in the nursing assistant program and I work with Leona. I mean, Dr. Guillano."

Marla didn't seem to notice the uneasiness Bella felt, standing there. The truth was, Bella didn't know how to act to being there with Leona. Would Marla think it odd that she was tagging along? Marla's eyes darted toward Brad, and Bella followed her gaze. He looked so at peace, and Marla clearly wasn't paying Bella any attention. Her fears slipped away.

"After you left, he stayed asleep."

"Glad to hear," Leona said. She walked over and knelt next to him, gently nudging him awake. "Time to go home," she said, her voice an airy whisper.

Bella watched as Brad opened his eyes and rubbed them. Leona helped him to his feet, and he opened his eyes wide enough to see Bella.

"Bella!" he exclaimed.

"Hey, bud." Bella pulled him into her arms. "I wanted to come see you."

"Thank you." He parted from the hug, then turned to Leona. "Mama Lona, are we going home?"

Bella grinned. Leona had the sweetest smile on her lips. "You bet we are," she said. "Say thank you to Marla."

Brad gave Marla his thanks as Leona reached down and picked up the sleeping bag. She started to fold it, but Marla spoke up. "Oh, that's not necessary. That's why I get paid here."

Leona laid the sleeping bag back down and walked over to Brad. She grabbed his hand, and the three of them said goodbye to Marla, then left the day care. "Did you have fun?" Leona asked.

"The best." He then frowned and glanced up at Leona. "I'm sorry I wouldn't go to sleep."

"Brad, you have nothing to apologize for."

Their interaction was cute, and Bella felt that Brad was in the perfect place with Leona. They both seemed to mesh so well together, and the conversation kept going the entire way to the parking lot. Once they reached the lot, Bella turned to Leona. She wasn't sure how they would explain to Brad that they would both be at the house, but Leona didn't even flinch.

"Are you going to follow me?" she asked.

Bella nodded, then turned to her car. She hurried over and got inside so that she wouldn't be left too far behind. She was able to keep up with Leona, and when they turned into the driveway, Bella parked along the street. She hesitated before walking up to meet Brad and Leona.

"Are you guys getting married?" Brad asked, once they got into the house.

Bella felt her cheeks getting excruciatingly hot. She looked over to Leona, but Leona had a smile that spread across her face. "That's a long way off, bud," she said, then giggled. "For now, just think of Bella as a friend who is visiting." She winked at Bella and Bella quickly looked away.

Being called just a friend stung, but she understood why Leona said it. Brad would be too confused about Bella otherwise. Still,

Bella couldn't help but think about marriage and a family. Was she ready for that so soon? The plan had always been to have kids when she was thirty.

"Let's get you up to bed," Leona said to Brad.

"Are you coming, Bella?" he asked, turning to face her.

"Um, I, I…"

"Come on, Bella." Leona said, reaching out for her hand. Bella took it, and they headed upstairs to Brad's room. Leona went through a couple of drawers until she found some clothes for Brad. "Get changed and we'll be in to kiss you goodnight."

Leona grabbed Bella's hand again and escorted her out of the room. When the door was closed, Bella glanced over at Leona. "A friend visiting, huh?" she teased.

Leona laughed. "Your face was a tinge red."

"Tinge?" Bella laughed, shaking her head. "I don't think I've ever been more uncomfortable in my life." She leaned back against the wall and stared at Leona.

"What made it more awkward? Him asking the question or you thinking about it?"

Bella shrugged. "Both, I suppose. Do you want marriage? Not with us…I mean, it's too soon. But someday. With someone, or…" She let her words fade, unsure how to salvage her rambling.

Leona reached up and brushed her hand over the side of Bella's face. "Yes. I've always wanted marriage and a family. Is this situation too much? If it is, we can put the brakes on—"

"No," Bella said, maybe a bit too forcefully. "I like whatever this is. It's not too much, only confusing. You know I want marriage and kids, but this isn't at all what I expected or planned for. And I don't want to confuse Brad when I'm still figuring my life out."

Leona brushed her lips against Bella's. "I know. I can't say I'll be happy with things like this forever because both Brad and I need stability, but for now, I'm happy."

"I promise I won't be so undecided forever."

"Good." Before Leona could thoroughly kiss Bella, the door opened. Bella quickly pulled back, and they both turned to look at Brad. "Let's get you in bed," Leona said.

Bella and Leona entered the room and Brad hopped into bed. "Nighty night, buddy."

"Night, Mama Lona." He wrapped his arms around her, and she kissed the top of his head. Bella then moved in and brushed her hand against Brad's forehead. "Night, Bella."

"Night, little guy," she responded, kissing his forehead.

He shifted onto his side and grabbed his teddy bear, holding it tightly to his chest. Bella and Leona stood at the door for a while, and then Leona turned and looked at her. Bella moved in and kissed her softly, going with her emotions, not allowing the feeling to pass.

When they parted, Leona smiled and reached for her hand, pulling her out of the room. They closed the door so that it was just slightly ajar. Leona pulled Bella toward another bedroom and Bella laughed, unable to keep up. Once they were inside Leona's room, Leona closed the door and locked it behind them. She grabbed the bottom of Bella's shirt and slowly pulled it up over her head. She tossed it to the side, and Bella unclasped her bra. When her bra dropped to the floor, she tugged at Leona's jacket and shirt until they were both off.

When they were both undressed from the top up, Leona pushed Bella toward the bed and Bella fell back against it. She looked up, her eyes gazing over Leona's breasts. Leona moved in and kissed her, and Bella tugged at her pants, removing them, then her panties, feeling the warmth in her nether regions. She pulled Leona down on top of her and they eagerly continued to kiss. Bella was no longer exhausted, and it was all because of Leona. The only thing that mattered in this moment was right in front of her.

———

Leona opened her mouth, just enough to allow Bella's tongue to enter. Bella felt like she no longer needed rest, as long as she was with Leona. She didn't even know what time it was as they continued to make out, the sun barely drifting through the bedroom window.

"I'd better go," Bella whispered. "Brad will be up at any moment, and frankly, I don't know that you're ready to have that conversation with him." She giggled, kissing Leona hard before pulling back.

Leona groaned, the sound echoing through the walls of her bedroom. Bella grabbed her bra and put it on, then noticed that Leona had her eyes directed toward her. "What are you smirking about?" Bella asked, pulling her top down over her.

"You're beautiful."

Bella felt her face get warm as she slipped on her panties and then her pants. Though she had never reacted when Jackson called her that, those words from Leona made her insides melt. "Well, thank you, but I don't quite know how to take your compliments."

Leona laughed loudly, then pushed herself up onto her hands, so that she was on all fours, hovering closer to Bella's lips. "A thank you will suffice." She kissed her softly, then fell back onto the bed and continued to stare at Bella as Bella put her socks and shoes on.

She hesitated, then looked over to Leona. "For the record, you're beautiful yourself."

Leona wiggled her eyebrows, then smiled. "For an older woman?"

Bella shrugged. "For any woman. Age is just a number, after

all." She walked over to Leona, as Leona's eyes followed her every move. Bella brushed her hand along Leona's cheek and kissed her. In any relationship, Bella was more the submissive type, scared to take the lead. When it came to Leona, she caught herself in many ways wanting to be the aggressor in the relationship, wanting to open herself to letting go fully. "I'll call you later, after school."

"I look forward to it," Leona said, grinning.

Bella waved goodbye and headed for the door. The moment she opened it, she came face to face with Brad. He had one arm raised, seemingly about to knock on the door. His eyes widened when he looked up and saw her. Bella glanced back toward the bed, where Leona had pulled the covers up tightly under her chin.

"Hey, Brad," Bella said.

"Hey." His wide-eyed expression turned into a smile. "You startled me." He laughed and Bella realized that he wasn't startled by the fact that she was there, but the fact that the door had opened just before he knocked.

"Sorry, bud." She ruffled his hair with her hands, then looked over at Leona, whose eyes were now completely bugged out. Bella turned back to Brad, asking, "Want to grab something to eat in the kitchen?"

"Yeah!" He reached for Bella's hand and practically pulled her down the stairs. Bella laughed as she scuffed down the stairs to get to the kitchen. "Mama Lona has these cinnamon muffins that taste like heaven." He shrugged. "Not that heaven has a taste, but I heard someone say it at the foster home."

Bella smirked. "Well, must be amazing, then. I'd love to taste those."

He pointed to the freezer and Bella made herself at home by taking them out and putting them into the microwave. Before they were done, Leona rushed into the kitchen. Her eyes were no longer filled with embarrassment and her cheeks had turned into a rosy hue.

"What are you both making in here?"

Brad propped himself against the counter. "Those muffins. They were so good." He enthusiastically rubbed his hands together.

When he wasn't paying attention, she looked over to Bella and mouthed, *Thank you.* Bella nodded as the microwave dinged and she pulled the muffins out. "Hmmmm…smells delish," she said. "And breakfast is served."

Despite her hesitancy, she stayed at the house and ate, immediately discovering how easy things were, being there with Brad and Leona. They were like the world's cutest little family, and Bella was finding it hard to leave.

She finally said her goodbyes and left, stopping on the porch. She couldn't remember the last time she had gone so long without checking her phone. Sure enough, the battery flashed red, signaling her phone was about to die. But just below it, she saw the slew of missed calls and texts from Jackson.

Jackson: Bella, I'm at your place. Are you working? Can we talk?

Jackson: Bella. I called the hospital and they said you aren't working tonight. I'm worried. Where are you?

Jackson: BELLA…

Jackson: If I don't hear from you in an hour, I'm calling the cops.

Bella counted a total of twelve missed calls. He had been silent a few days after she had told him she wanted a break, then he had started messaging her more and more. She felt guilty, but why couldn't he give her the space she had told him she needed? Bella groaned and pulled up his phone number. She hit the Call button, but before it started ringing, her phone died.

"Great," she mumbled. She went to her car and dug in her middle console for her charger, but she couldn't find it amid her CDs, business cards, and other trash that crowded the console. She put her key in the ignition and started the car. Since she had some time, she figured she needed to go talk to Jackson in person. Maybe it would help him give her more space and time to consider her options. She still cared for Jackson, but the more time she spent with Leona, the more her heart was with her.

Thirty minutes later, Bella turned down Jackson's road. As she drew closer, she saw his truck parked in the driveway. She was sure she would feel much better the moment she got this off her chest. But when she stood at his door, the nerves came rushing back in. She stepped to the side and looked into the window, where she could see her reflection. Her hair was all frazzled. She hadn't even taken the time to brush it.

Bella sighed and tried to straighten her hair—as if that would relieve her nerves. "He's not going to care what you look like, Bella. By the sound of the texts, he was probably panicking." She cringed, hoping that he hadn't rushed to call the cops.

Getting cold feet, she turned away from the door, her eyes turning to Jackson's truck. She stared at it, trying to build her resolve. "I can't just leave now." There was a hitch in her throat as a lump grew. "You've got this, Bella. He's the person you've always known. Just be honest with him."

Bella turned around and marched back up to his door, knocking before she could change her mind again. *Come on. Answer the door.* After a few more minutes, she rang the doorbell, then knocked again. Ten minutes passed by, and Bella stood there, a bit confused. Again, she knocked. She waited another five minutes before giving up. His car was there, but maybe it was broken down. But if he wasn't home, then there was only one other place to check.

Bella got back in her car and stared at her rearview mirror. She still looked awful. Did she want to rush to the jewelry store when other customers could easily be there? She started the car and backed up. It beat the alternative—running home when she knew that she would find reasons to panic over where Jackson could be. The sooner she talked to him, the better she would be for it.

Several cars were already there when she turned into the store's parking lot. Again, she gave herself a onceover, trying her best to fix herself so that when she walked into the store, she would look at least a little put together. She smoothed her hair again. *Good enough, I guess.*

The bell hanging on the door rang as she entered. Two people stood at a counter, with a clerk hovering over them. When Nelly looked up, she greeted Bella with a grin. "Hey, B, I'll be with you shortly." She always liked to greet people in rhyme, or as much of a rhyme as she could.

Another couple glanced at a case full of bracelets. A third couple stood at a case full of diamonds. Bella looked between the couples and smiled to herself. They all seemed happy. It was already a busy morning, and frankly, Bella considered just ducking out of there and worrying about seeing Jackson later.

The bell sounded again, and she looked over to see a man enter the shop and head straight for the case of rings, like he was a man on a mission. There was a time when Bella dreamed that Jackson would have been that man. But now, she had to admit that she was relieved they hadn't taken their relationship further.

"What can I do for you?" Nelly asked, approaching Bella from the side.

Bella looked around the swamped room. "Are you alone?"

She grimaced and nodded. "Camryn called in sick and couldn't get a replacement. Don't you worry, though. These people have all been waited on."

"Except for that guy," Bella said, nodding toward the man.

She laughed and rolled her eyes. "Mr. Snooty, you mean? He comes in at least three times a week, looks in the case, tosses his nose up, and leaves. Just can't find what he's looking for, I suppose."

"And he keeps coming back? Isn't it clear that maybe this store doesn't have what he wants?"

She laughed. "You would think, huh?" She shook her head. "He just doesn't want to give up hope, I guess. But you didn't come to talk about him, I'm sure. What's up?"

Bella looked around the store. "Just here to see Jackson. He should be out here giving you a hand. Is he hiding in the back somewhere?"

Nelly frowned. "No, he's not here. He's out of town for a few days. Said he needed a vacay or something. Called this morning and left a message. Just assumed you'd know."

Bella frowned, then pretended she had forgotten. "Oh, of course. Silly me." She playfully slapped her forehead. "Work has been crazy, and it slipped my mind."

"Miss? I would like to see this ring please."

Both Bella and Nelly turned to the guy that Nelly had called Mr. Snooty. Nelly's eyes widened, and she threw a side-glance to Bella. "I'll be right with you. Um, I have to go, Bella. See ya." She hurried away, leaving Bella confused.

Bella left the store and thought back to Nelly's words. For one, Jackson's car was definitely in the driveway. Another thing that had her concerned was that in all those texts Jackson had sent her, he had never once mentioned a vacation. She frowned, walking back to the car and finally getting in the driver's seat. What was going on? She only hoped Jackson was okay.

CHAPTER SEVENTEEN

Leona

"Now, are youe sure you want to go to school?" Leona asked, turning to face Brad.

He had a sweet grin on his face, and he quickly nodded. Leona looked up to the school; it seemed so big. Was he ready for kindergarten? She turned back to him and knelt at his level, drawing his eyes back to her. "No one will be upset with you if you've changed your mind."

He released a groan, which made her laugh. "Mama Lona, I want to go. Please." He clasped his hands together. The truth was that sending him to school could be a saving grace for her. If he were at school while she worked, then she wouldn't have to leave him at the day care. With her schedule, she was sure she could work it out to make sure she got him to and from school, even if that meant hiring a nanny who could handle some of the transporting.

She stood up and grabbed his hand. He was ready, but Leona

wasn't. It didn't feel like they had been together long enough for her to usher him off to school so suddenly. But, in a way, she understood his need and desire to be with other kids his age. It just felt like a stepping-stone to him getting older already. It really was true what people said about kids growing up so fast.

They entered the building and Leona looked around for the office. There wasn't a huge sign that showed people where to go, even though she thought there should be. She finally found a woman walking down a hallway, headed toward the front door.

"Excuse me," she said, her voice coming out a bit more forceful than she had intended. The woman stopped and arched an eyebrow, then tossed a look down to Brad.

"Yes?" she asked, looking back up and meeting Leona's gaze.

"We're looking for the registration office."

"Just head down this hallway. It's the first door on the right. You'll see a big sign that reads 'office.'"

Leona gave a weak smile. It was exactly the sign she was looking for. She had just thought it would be closer to the front door. "Thank you."

The woman nodded, then disappeared. Leona looked down at Brad, who was ready to pull her down the hallway, but Leona dug her heels into the floor. "I'll give you one more shot to change your mind."

"Mama Lona!" he groaned, tossing her an exasperated look. Leona shrugged. She had to try, at least.

They got to the office and Leona released a breath. Why was she so nervous? It was the same question she had asked herself a million times over, but now that the moment was upon them, her heart was palpitating heavily. It was crazy. It wasn't like he was going off to college or getting married. She couldn't even imagine that happening.

A woman behind the desk greeted them with a bright and easy smile. "Hello, may I help you?"

She caught the woman's name on a desk name tag. "Hi, Melody," Leona began. "I spoke with a Charmaine Allo yesterday afternoon and she's expecting Brad Carver to come into the building today. He's starting kindergarten."

She smiled. "Are you nervous?" the woman asked.

Leona laughed. "How could you tell?"

"I've been around the block a few times. I know several parents who have panic attacks dropping their kids off here. It's cute. I'm not a mother so I wouldn't know the feeling, but you're giving off that vibe. Don't you worry, though. Brad will be well taken care of."

That warmed Leona's heart, and she nodded, her panic slightly dissipating.

Melody continued, "She's waiting for you back in that office. Go ahead and head on in."

"Thank you," Leona said gratefully.

She continued to hold on to Brad's hand as she led him through the doors. A woman looked up and stood up from her desk. "Leona Guillano?" she asked.

"Right. And this is Brad." She presented him, pressing her hand against his back.

"How are you, Brad?" Charmaine held out her hand to him and he shook it with no hesitation. He was excited for this moment, while Leona was doing her best to avoid it. She shook her head, not sure why he was so confident.

"I'm good. Are there lots of kids here?" he asked, hope shining in his eyes.

Leona smiled as Charmaine spoke to him like he was an adult. It eased Leona's mind. After they finished talking, she turned to Leona.

"There are a few papers I need you to sign. We're working with the children's home on getting his papers, birth certificate, etcetera. But we'll get all that sorted on our end."

"Sounds good," Leona replied, swallowing the lump again. Charmaine pushed some papers toward her and Leona saw her hands shaking as she tried to sign her name. Charmaine reached out and touched her hand.

"He's going to be fine," she said reassuringly.

Leona laughed. "He will, but I'm a nervous wreck." She shrugged. "Guess it has to be done." She released a breath and went back to signing the forms. Then it was done, and she was turned away from Brad's grasp. She thought the whole thing would be a longer process, but it had only been a mere twenty minutes before a woman escorted Brad away from Leona. She waved to him until he disappeared around the corner.

Leona looked over to Charmaine, who reached out and touched Leona's arm. "You're not the first person to get emotional in seeing your child go off to his first day of school. He's in good hands, though. And you're doing a great thing in fostering him. Foster kids need great families to be a part of, and I can tell you're one of the best."

"Thank you." Leona backed away from her, still feeling uneasy, but hoping that feeling would dissipate.

"We'll call you if we need anything," Charmaine continued.

Leona nodded, then turned and left the office. She made it to her car before she broke down. Brad looked way too small to be heading off to a place where she couldn't look after him. When she finally regained her composure, she straightened up and pulled out of the parking spot. She was going to have to make it through the day at work. In that moment, she wasn't sure she could. The only thing that brought her comfort was the knowledge that Bella would be there at work.

While they hadn't talked much since Bella had left her house the previous morning, Leona was ready to share some intimate moments locked away in the hospital rooms. It was something that kept a smile on her face.

When she got to the hospital, she took the elevator, hoping that Bella would greet her the moment she stepped onto the floor. That didn't happen, but she continued to look for her until she walked to her office. She was probably tucked in a patient's room. In no time, she would have a real encounter with Bella, and she couldn't wait for that to happen.

LEONA LOOKED UP AND DOWN THE HALLWAYS, TRYING TO find Bella. Was Bella intentionally dodging her this morning? It felt like it was a very real possibility. After the night they had spent together, she felt it was only right that they would want to share a few stolen moments. The couple of times they had talked on the phone the previous night, Brad was there to listen to the conversations. Now that she was at work, she wanted that intimate time together. But the only time she was able to see Bella was when they had to work together to take care of a few patients. Not even once did Bella look like she wanted to steal away with Leona.

Jacqueline was sitting at the desk when Leona approached her. She looked up and jumped up from her chair. "Hi, Dr. Guillano." She was always eager to look like she did no wrong, but Leona couldn't let her believe that anytime soon. Even though she wasn't going to confront Jacqueline about what she did, she wasn't going to make things easy on her.

"Have you seen Bella?" Leona asked, keeping the question short and to the point.

Jacqueline lowered herself down into a chair. "She said she was going to stock some shelves. I offered to help, but she said she needed some time alone." She shrugged. "Last I saw her, she was in that stockroom." She pointed toward the room closest to them.

"Thanks," Leona walked over to the room and went to open the door, but it was locked. She jiggled the knob for a moment, then leaned against the door. "Bella, it's Leona. Are you in there?"

The handle turned and then the door pushed open. Leona slipped inside and locked the door behind her. She turned to see Bella sitting on the floor. Bella looked away, but it was too late. Leona saw she had been crying.

"Bella!" she exclaimed. She moved in and sat down next to her. "What's wrong?"

Bella held up her phone, finally looking in her direction. "This is what's wrong. I've tried calling Jackson two dozen times, and he's ignoring my calls. The calls are going straight to voicemail. It makes no sense."

She pushed a button and put the call on speaker. A man's voice came on the phone, asking them to leave a message. She disconnected the call and shook her head. "I know we're on a break, but I can't help worrying. He's been acting strange and a little desperate lately. I worry that I broke his heart and...I don't know. I'm feeling a lot of guilt right now."

"Maybe you should start at the beginning," Leona murmured.

She sighed and looked over to Leona. "Yesterday after I left your house, I saw I had missed calls and texts from him. He seemed concerned, so I decided that we needed to talk in person so I could just be open and honest with him about everything. I feel I owe him that much, so I went to his house."

As Bella continued, Leona listened. She nodded when it seemed right and sighed when it felt like that was what she needed to do.

"I don't know. It makes no sense why he won't answer my

calls." Bella slipped her phone into her pocket, sighing. "I can see you looking at me like that. I told him we're on a break and he can do whatever he wants to do. I have this strange feeling though. What if...What if he's had someone on the side for months and I just never knew about it? Part of me is worried he's hurt, and the other part is worried he was cheating."

Leona shook her head. "I'm not looking at you in any way. You guys have a history, so I can understand your concern about him. I get it."

Bella looked up. "Even though I haven't been exactly innocent? We kissed before I went on a break from him."

Leona smiled. "What I've realized through the years of my life is that the heart wants what it wants. You can't curse yourself for that."

"You don't think I'm being crazy?"

Leona shrugged, though there was a part of her that wondered why Bella seemed so upset about it. If she was sure that she had made the right choice, then why would it matter if Jackson had moved on as well? Maybe it was only the thought that he'd been unfaithful while they were still together. "I think you're being exactly how you feel. No one can fault you on what's weighing on your heart."

Bella looked up and Leona reached out and touched her hair, then withdrew her hand. "I know I've been uncertain, but I've been thinking a lot about everything since I left your house. I'm where I want to be," Bella quietly spoke. "I want us to give this a try. I just wish I could talk to Jackson and tell him where my heart is. I hope you understand that."

Leona nodded. "Again, I won't fault you for how you feel, and I'm happy to hear that you're feeling more confident about what you want. I want us to give this a try, too. Maybe this is the absolute wrong time to say this or even suggest it, but I was hoping you would want to go out to dinner tonight. You, me, and Brad. Nothing too fancy. I thought about getting someone to watch him, but I took him to school today and thought it could be a celebration of his first day. If that's stupid, then forget I even said it."

Before Leona could say anything else, Bella moved in and claimed Leona's lips into a heated kiss, giving Leona her answer. Despite how Bella felt in that supply closet, she didn't regret being with Leona, and that was what mattered most. They would continue to see where things could go.

CHAPTER EIGHTEEN

Bella

"Hello, you've reached Jackson. As you can see, I'm not available to take your call. You know what to do. I'll return your call as soon as I can."

"Jackson, it's Bella. Again. I've only tried calling you a million times and you're not picking up. We really need to talk. Call me." Bella disconnected the call as her doorbell rang. She glanced at her reflection and scrunched up her nose. She had an idea of what she wanted to wear but she had torn through her closet, and nothing seemed to suit the mood of the evening.

She went to the front door and opened it. Her eyes looked over the outfit Leona wore, and her face went pale. "Excuse me while I go change," she mumbled.

Leona laughed and grabbed her hand, pulling her toward her. Bella's lips brushed against Leona's. "You look beautiful," Leona said.

Bella grimaced. "I'm underdressed."

Leona stood at her door wearing a floral dress. Bella had never seen her dressed in anything but work attire, so this was all new for her. The way Leona trailed her eyes over her body, she knew she shouldn't be concerned about the blouse and jeans she wore. Still, she felt like a sore thumb next to Leona.

For the first time, Brad cleared his throat and Bella looked down to glance at him. She had forgotten he was even there. He had a sneaky grin and looked up at Bella. "Hey, Brad!" she said, giving him a high-five.

"Hi Bella. I'm with Mama Lona. You look beautiful."

Bella blushed and fought hard not to pick him up in her arms and twirl him around the floor. That was the sweetest thing he could have said to her in that very moment. "Thank you, and you are a sweetheart for saying that. Just for that, you can choose where we go to eat."

"Rocket Place!" he exclaimed.

Leona laughed. "You really shouldn't have let him choose. Now we'll have to sit in those little rocket ships."

Bella grinned. As long as she was with them, she didn't care. "Looking forward to it," she said.

With that, they left her apartment and got into Leona's vehicle. The whole ride to the restaurant, Brad kept up a stream of chatter from the backseat. Bella caught herself looking over at Leona. She had the sweetest smile on her face. When they were nearly at the restaurant, Leona reached out for her hand, and that was how they rode the rest of the way there.

Bella was getting more confident in her choices, more comfortable with letting her life plan pivot. Though they weren't officially a couple, Bella was moving more and more in that direction. She only hoped she wasn't ultimately making the wrong decision, and that things with her and Leona wouldn't fall apart. Jackson had been a sure thing. What she had with Leona still felt rocky for some reason.

Leona turned into the parking lot and Bella's jaw dropped. "Is this place always this busy?" Bella asked.

Leona laughed. "Your guess is as good as mine. I've never been here, but it seems like the place to be on a Thursday night."

"That's Maxine," Brad hollered from the backseat. Bella looked over her shoulder to see him pointing out the window.

"A school classmate?" Bella asked.

He nodded. "She's nice."

Bella grinned and looked over to Leona. "Looks like he's already making friends after just one day. Can't get any better than that."

Leona nodded happily. She looked over her shoulder to Brad. "Are you ready to go?"

He was already hopping out of his booster seat. They all got out of the car and headed up to the front door. When Brad tried to run ahead, Leona quickly grabbed his hand and pulled him back to them. Leona was the motherly type, and it impressed Bella how well she seemed to have jumped into the role, like she was meant to do it her entire life.

Bella grabbed the door and waited for Leona and Brad to step into the building first before she joined them. Brad looked around the restaurant, then he pointed to the corner. "She's sitting over there. Can we go over there?"

"We don't want to bother them, but we'll go grab the ship right next to them." Leona grinned when she looked to Bella. "Words I never thought I'd be saying on a date."

We're on a date, Bella thought gleefully. It calmed her nerves that she didn't have to worry about where the evening could wind up. The three of them headed over to the ship and Brad eagerly waved when Maxine looked in their direction. "Hey, Brad!" Maxine called.

Bella and Leona took one side and Brad slid into the spot across from them. He kept looking over his shoulder to where Maxine sat with her parents. Or, at least Bella assumed they were her parents. She looked over to Leona and gently squeezed her hand. "I think maybe your boy has a crush."

Leona laughed. "Looks that way, doesn't it?" she whispered.

They grabbed their menus and looked through them, waiting for the waitress. Within five minutes they had placed their orders and were sipping on their drinks. "How was your first day at school, Brad?" Bella asked. "What'd you do?"

"Lots of coloring," he said. "They have a board at the front of the class and if you draw a picture the teacher will show…show…" He hesitated. "She said she would do something and used a word. Show something."

"Showcase?" Leona asked.

His eyes lit up and nodded. "Yep. That's what she said."

"You're so smart," Bella teased.

Leona laughed. "The teacher sent home a notebook of things that she does in the class. That was one of the things she mentioned."

Bella reached under the table and took her hand into hers. Leona's grin widened across her face as they held one another's hand and continued their conversation with Brad.

"Mama Lona?" Brad asked.

"Yes, bud?"

"There's going to be a meeting at the school and your presence is required."

Leona snickered. "My presence?"

"That's what the teacher said. Something about seeing everything your kid has accomplished. I'll be bringing papers home about it."

"Just don't forget," Leona said.

He shook his head. "I won't."

Their pizza came, and they took a moment to appreciate the food. A few times, Brad spoke up, and either Leona or Bella would respond, but the conversation soon died to a small murmur as they all focused on their meal.

Bella nodded, taking a bite of the pizza. "This pizza isn't bad. I'll have to remember this place."

"It's hard to miss," Leona teased. That brought a giggle to Bella's lips, and they continued to eat.

"I'm stuffed," Brad moaned.

"Well, you did have three slices and two crazy breads. I'm not surprised. That's a lot of food for such a little guy."

He grinned. "I was hungry, and it was good."

Bella nodded. "Agreed on both parts."

Maxine approached their table, smiling shyly. "Brad? You wanna go play some games?"

Brad sat up in the spaceship and looked over to Leona. "Mama Lona, can I?" he asked.

Bella watched as Leona dug some money out of her purse and handed it over to him. "Enjoy yourself," she said.

"Thank you!" He jumped up and both kids ran off.

Bella laughed and Leona raised an eyebrow. "You're going to have that boy wrapped around your finger. You know that, right?"

Leona snickered. "I wouldn't have it any other way."

Leona beamed with happiness as she watched Brad play with his new friend. Bella was glad that Leona had Brad in her life because everyone deserved something to make their hearts shine, and Leona had found that. More and more, Bella wanted to be another reason Leona's heart shone.

BELLA LOOKED OVER TO WHERE BRAD WAS TOSSING SOME basketballs into a hoop. She had moved to the spot where Brad had sat earlier, and she felt Leona's steady gaze on her. Bella looked over and smiled at her. "He's having the time of his life," she said.

"That he is. But what about you?"

Bella smirked. "I can't complain. This is a beautiful place to have our first date."

Leona laughed. "Well, typically I like to shoot for higher standards, but this place does have a cool vibe. Don't you think?"

Bella chuckled. "Very cool." She sipped on her Coke and dropped her eyes to the tray of pizza. They still had enough to make out a second helping for all. The restaurant didn't disappoint with their portions.

"Have you talked to your boyfriend?" Leona suddenly blurted.

Bella looked up, a little startled, and Leona closed her mouth and shook her head. "None of my business. I just saw how upset you were and wondered if things had gotten resolved. You don't have to tell me if you don't want to, though."

Bella leaned back in her booth and waited for her to finish speaking. "Are you done?" she asked, grinning. "If you are, then I can tell you my response. Then again, if you want to ramble for another fifteen minutes, we can discuss it after that."

Leona's eyes widened, then fell. "Just nervous."

"Clearly. Well, truth is, no, I haven't talked to him. It's not because I haven't tried. He's been ignoring my calls."

"Is that usual?"

Bella shook her head. "Could be that he's trying to give me a taste of my own medicine. Who knows? I don't want to think about him tonight, though. I want to think about life beyond Jackson. And there is life beyond him. I know that now." She reached across the table and took Leona's hand in hers. "I didn't realize the happiness I was allowed to have until I started spending time with you."

"Which has only just begun, I hope." Leona winked at her, and Bella felt her cheeks flush.

"Mama Lona," Brad said, coming up to their table. Instinctively, she pulled her hand back from Leona's. She didn't want Brad to feel awkward with them being intimate, but it was only her paranoia. Brad had a grin that didn't quit. "I'm tired."

"You've been playing for a long time," Leona said. "Let's get you home and ready for bed."

Leona reached in her purse to grab her wallet but Bella tossed some bills onto the table. "You're not paying," Leona argued.

"Please." Bella tilted her head. "I want to treat. This was a big day for Brad, and I want to celebrate that. You can get next time."

Leona gave her a soft smile and dropped her wallet back in her purse. That was one win for Bella, but she didn't think there would be many more to come. Leona was the type that usually got her way, being the strong and independent woman she was.

As they drove toward the house, it started to rain slowly, then picked up in speed and intensity. It soon got to the point that Leona was slowing her speed and trying to look around the windshield wipers.

"We can pull off and stop," Bella whispered. "Wait for the rain to stop, if you want."

Leona shook her head. "We're fine. We're almost to the house." Bella glanced over her shoulder at Brad. His eyes were wide as he stared out the window.

"What did you like most about school today?" Bella asked, attempting to take his mind off the rain outside.

"Um…coloring." A loud crack of thunder sounded, shaking the car. "Ahhhh!" he screamed.

"It's fine, Brad. That's just the thunder talking to the lightning. That's what my folks always say, especially my mother."

Brad nodded, seemingly calmed down by those words. A few minutes later, Leona pulled into the driveway.

"Do you have umbrellas?" Bella asked.

"They're somewhere around here. Or we could run…" She looked over her shoulder and Bella glanced behind her. Brad nodded, eager to get inside.

"Get ready," Leona called. Brad unbuckled his seat and then they all grabbed for their doors. "Run!" she hollered.

The three of them opened their doors and ran for their lives to reach the front door. By the time they reached the porch, they were in a fit of giggles and soaked down to their underwear.

"This is the best night of my life," Brad spoke between giggles. He threw his arms around Leona, and they embraced for a moment. It was so heartfelt, Bella felt tears sting at her eyes. How much sweeter could the evening get?

They parted from their embrace and Leona unlocked the doors for them to enter the house. Bella stood back, feeling it was fitting that she allowed the two of them to have this moment together. "I think I'm going to start a fire," she said, moving toward the living room.

Leona looked over and frowned. "Are you sure? You're welcome to come upstairs."

Bella shook her head. "I'm positive. You two enjoy your time together." She entered the living room and went over to the fireplace. Everything was already set out for the fire, so she worked on getting that going.

She would always have time to spend with Leona, but it was time that Leona took the moments she could with Brad and made the best of every minute they had together.

CHAPTER NINETEEN

Leona

arm water washed over Leona's body. She could still smell Bella's scent on her from the two of them repeatedly exploring one another the previous night, first in front of the fireplace and then in her bed. Time after time after time. A smile broadened across her face. If she could have nights like that forever, she would die a very happy woman.

I need to get home and get changed for class. I'm not doing well in anatomy, or else I would gladly miss the class. Tell Brad I said goodbye.

Those words still rung in her ears. She just wanted to be near Bella every second of every day, but time didn't allow for that. Her phone started ringing, and she groaned and peeked her head out of the shower. It was the hospital, so she quickly turned the water off and answered the phone.

"Hello?"

"Dr. Guillano? This is Tori. I was asked to call you because Dr.

Whalen is out sick and there isn't another doctor to cover the shift. They were wondering if you could come in."

Leona looked down at her wet body. The last place she wanted to be was the hospital, when she knew that Jacqueline would most likely be the nurse she would be set to work with. That would make for some awkwardness. But she couldn't imagine leaving the ward not well-staffed.

"I have to get Brad to school and then I can be there. Nine o'clock, maybe?"

"That would be great. Thank you so much. We all appreciate this."

"Not a problem. See you then." Leona disconnected the call and stepped back into the shower to finish up. When she turned the water back on, she couldn't get the hot water to kick in, so she was left with a cold and miserable ending to her shower, but she made do with it.

She got out of the shower and dressed, then brushed her teeth and did her hair. When she got out into the hall and to Brad's room, she saw that he was finishing up getting ready as well.

"How do I look?" he asked.

Leona laughed. Despite having two different shoes on, he didn't look half bad. "You look great. But maybe we should try to match the shoes this time. She reached under his bed and pulled out another Teenage Mutant Ninja Turtle shoe.

He giggled. "There it is."

He grabbed it from her and sat down on the floor, changing out his shoes. "I'm going to run down and make breakfast for us. I just got called into work, so I need to get you to school before heading to the hospital. Does cereal sound okay? Or would you rather have oatmeal?"

"Do you have blueberries in the oatmeal?" he asked.

Leona grinned. "I can make that happen, if that's what you want."

"Yes, please." He continued to change his shoes as she left the room and went to the kitchen to make his oatmeal. As she headed toward the cupboards, she saw a note in the middle of the table. She picked it up and read it, a smile blossoming on her face.

Leona and Brad —

I had a great time last night. Looking forward to doing it again soon!

Bella

Leona held the note to her heart. Bella knew just how to bring a smile to her face. And the fact that she had included Brad only made it that much more special. She heard Brad's feet on the stairs, and she turned to look at him when he entered the kitchen.

"Bella left us a note." She handed the note to him.

"What's it say? I can't read. Not really. But I can make stuff up." He laughed. Leona took the note and read it to him. Brad grinned. "I had a good time, too."

"So did I," Leona admitted. She popped two bowls of oatmeal into the microwave, then grabbed some blueberries from the fridge. When the microwave dinged, she poured some blueberries in and mixed them up fully. "Try that," she said, passing one of the bowls and a spoon to Brad.

"Yummy," he said.

Leona smirked and took a bite of her own. It wasn't bad, but it wasn't some delicious meal she had slaved over the stove to make. Still, it seemed to be enough for Brad. She grabbed some orange juice and poured two glasses.

They finished their breakfast in record time so that Leona could drop Brad off and head to work. Fifteen minutes before he had to be at school, she grabbed her purse. "Are you ready?" she asked.

He jumped down from his booster chair, and they were out the door and into the car. "Mama Lona," he said as they rounded the corner.

"Yes?" She looked in the rearview mirror and stared at him from the backseat.

"I was wondering if I could go in by myself. The other kids don't have an adult with them."

"Are you sure?" she asked, not comfortable with that in any way. Brad eagerly nodded his head.

"I'll be fine." She turned into the parking lot and followed the path of arrows that showed where people could drop off their kids. There were already a few people there, and they followed slowly behind the cars in front of them.

When it was finally their turn, Brad got out of his seat and opened the door. He looked over and waved to her. "Bye, Mama Lona," he called. He grabbed his backpack and headed away from the car. She stared after him, a tear sneaking its way down her cheek. A car honked behind her, and she glanced in the rearview mirror and gave a small wave before pulling away from the curb.

He didn't need her already. How sad was that? Leona had to remind herself that he was bound to be independent eventually. That thought did somehow calm her, if only slightly.

When she turned into the hospital's parking lot, she was no longer thinking negatively about those feelings. She grabbed her phone and pulled up her text messages.

Bella, just wanted to let you know that I was called into work. I know this is a huge ask but would you pick up Brad and bring him to the hospital? It's likely going to be a long day. Dr. Whalen is sick and I'm not sure when coverage will be in. If you can't, then I completely understand. 3:00, though, if you can. Just let me know. PS. That note you wrote us this morning was super sweet.

When she was satisfied with the text, she signed off with a single heart, then slipped her phone back into her purse. Leona got out of the car and headed up to the hospital, humming when she entered the elevator. Everything was working out just perfectly.

She should have assumed that would be the moment when everything was going to fall apart. As she stepped off the elevator, her eyes went straight to the desk. Standing there, a smile on her lips, was Cicily. But why? And what did she want now?

CHAPTER TWENTY

Bella

B ella fell on the couch and closed her eyes, immediately seeing Leona's smiling face playing like a video through her memory. She warmed up every time she was with Leona. When they had sex, she felt like they were one body orgasming together. It was how she always desired lovemaking to be.

Her eyes shot open. *Love?* That was the one word that continuously played through her mind when she thought about and pictured Leona. Slowly, she had fallen in love with Leona, and that startled her because she had spent so much time believing Jackson would be her future spouse.

She jumped up from the couch and went over to her bag of books. If she kept thinking about this, she would be late to class. The last thing she needed was a lecture from Professor Finch on being tardy and the art of making good grades. She still wasn't fully over the embarrassment of messing up by falling asleep in his class.

She grabbed her backpack and tossed it over her shoulder, then went to the door. When she opened it, her jaw dropped. Standing on the porch was Jackson. He had been pacing back and forth in front of the door. Who knew for how long? She gawked at him until he turned and faced her.

"Hey, Bella." This was the first time in what felt like forever that he didn't call her babe.

"Jackson!"

"Got your message. And you're right. We do need to talk. May I come in?"

It was the best time to have things out and speak from her heart, but she couldn't right now. "No," she said. His jaw dropped. "It's not that I don't want you to come in, but I have to get to school. Professor Finch already has it out for me, and I really don't want to give him any more reasons to hate me."

He smiled lightly, his jaw relaxing. "I doubt anyone could hate you."

So he didn't hate her. That was something.

"I want us to talk, Jackson. This isn't me making an excuse, I swear. But…" She adjusted her bag on her shoulder and looked up into his eyes. "If I miss class, I could ruin my chances of graduating. And I think we both know that would not be a good thing."

"No, of course not. I should have figured that you would be rushing off someplace. After all, it's how you've been the past couple of months. So, by all means…" He stepped aside and Bella closed the door behind her. She hesitated and looked back at him. His eyes were sullen and his mouth was in a downward frown.

She walked over to him and wrapped her arm around him, which made him straighten. "It's good to see you, Jackson." She softly kissed his cheek, then turned and left him.

She didn't want him to feel like she was abandoning him. But something had broken them, and it wasn't just because Bella had met Leona. She had never truly loved Jackson, and she had been too focused on her life falling into some perfect plan. She now realized how silly she had been. She had wanted to settle for a life that didn't fill her with passion and excitement, like the way she felt around Leona. How silly of her. Yes, she wanted to prove herself, but she'd carried a chip on her shoulder for too long. She had let her bullies affect her life for too many years. She was different now, and everything about her future was brighter.

It was a future with Leona and Brad, if Leona decided she wanted Bella to be a part of his life in that way. She would be a mom sooner than she expected, but screw the plan. Life was better this way, and she was now open to all of its wonderful possibilities.

She drove to school, trying to put Jackson out of her mind, but the further she got from her apartment, the harder it was to focus on anything but him. She was ready to tell him everything, and she had thought her resolve would make it easier, but Jackson was there, resting in her mind. She pulled into the parking lot, but there was a heaviness in her heart, which nearly caused her to turn around and head straight back to find him, hoping that he was still at her apartment waiting for her.

You have to go to class, Bella. You know this.

Bella forced herself out of the car and walked the long distance to the classroom. When she reached her class, she saw the room had already quickly filled up. Professor Finch stood at the front of the class, his back to the students. If she hurried, she could slip inside and go unnoticed. She hoped.

When she entered the room, though, it was like a loud horn had blared, signaling she had arrived. The professor turned and gazed toward her. "Ms. Strong," he said.

"Good morning, Professor Finch." She tried to move past him, but he wasn't through with her.

"I hope you remembered there would be a pop quiz today, and that you have studied fruitfully."

Bella nodded, her stomach going weak. Had he mentioned a quiz? She didn't recall, but she forced a smile. "Of course. I'm better prepared than I've been for any quiz in my life."

What was the quiz even about? She racked her brain, but nothing came to her.

Professor Finch tilted his head. "Interesting," he said. "There is a quiz, but I hadn't mentioned it to the class. But if you've been studying the whole book, I would say you're well-prepared." He smirked, and Bella's heart sunk.

Was he just out to get her? If that was the case, then why?

"I can assure you I have this down." She turned and stomped up the stairs to her seat.

Nowhere was it mentioned in the school manual that there would be one professor who knew the exact words to say to humiliate their students. But Bella knew she was stuck with Professor Finch, and now she had to worry about one more thing—passing a quiz.

———

FREEDOM, AT LAST. BELLA GRABBED HER BOOKS AND TOSSED them in her bag, anxious to get out of the classroom and as far away from Professor Finch as possible. His quiz hadn't disappointed. It was as tough as she would have expected to find in a master-level course. She just didn't want to think about how badly she'd bombed it, at least until the next week.

"Ms. Strong," Professor Finch spoke, his voice booming over the sound of shoes hitting the laminate flooring. She looked around, her heart sinking. She had been only two seconds from exiting and not having to look back.

"Yes, Professor Finch," she stated.

He continued to look down at some papers in front of him. "Thought we could finish our conversation from earlier."

"Our conversation?" Bella asked. He looked up and nodded, causing her to fidget from one foot to the other. "I thought we were done." Perhaps that was wishful thinking on her part, but she didn't know what else they possibly had to discuss.

"I was just about to grade your quiz. Would you care to wait?"

Bella dropped her gaze. *Not particularly.* She would have been just fine never to have to see the quiz again. And having him grade it in front of her? She could only imagine the horror of that.

"Well, I have another class to get to," she argued. It was a lie, of course, but what he didn't know wouldn't hurt her. She started to back away, but he looked back down at the pile of papers.

"It won't take much more than a minute." He skimmed over the quiz, and she watched as he took his red pen and marked off a point, then another, then another. She looked down at the floor, not able to stand watching him take more points off. The only thing she was relieved about was that he hadn't chosen to do this in front of the rest of the class. At least he had left her with some dignity.

After a minute ticked by, Professor Finch looked up and handed over her quiz. "Tsk tsk...I don't know what to tell you, Bella, but you had some promise and potential when you first came into the program. Now it just seems like you've gone downhill."

"Sir, I've been under some stress," Bella argued. "You know, with work and everything, it's just been a lot. I will do better. I can promise you that."

"Don't promise *me* anything. You need to make that promise to yourself. If your grades continue in this fashion, you're likely to take the semester over."

Her jaw dropped. "This is my last semester. If I have to take it over, I won't be able to graduate in May with everyone else. Please, don't say that's a possibility."

He shrugged. "That's up to you, but time is running out. I advise you to put everything on hold and focus solely on your classes."

Bella looked down. "I have to work to pay for my bills. That's non-negotiable."

He got up from his stool. "There's not much I can do. Your grade right now could give you a C, at best. You need a B to pass this semester. That means getting an A on every assignment and every quiz and test." Professor Finch heaved a sigh. "You're free to go."

Bella continued to stand there, her mind racing as she thought of various scenarios that could get her through. "Surely you have extra credit I could do. I *will* do whatever it takes to pass this class. I'm a hard worker, Professor Finch. Just give me a chance."

He looked over to her. "Fine, I'll give you an assignment." He walked back over to his podium and rifled through some folders. "Write a five-to-seven-page report on this topic." He handed a sheet of paper over to Bella and she stared at it.

"Artificial hearts?"

He nodded. "If you can get it to me by Monday morning, before the start of my first class at eight o'clock, I will grade it before your class. If I feel it's an A-worthy paper, then you'll have a better shot of passing this class."

"I won't disappoint you," she said, tucking the papers he handed her into her bag.

"I'm sure you won't. Now, good day."

Bella turned and left the classroom, already feeling discouraged, but she had to push herself. Over the weekend, she would get the assignment done and exceed his expectations. It was her best shot to making it through the semester and on to graduation.

CHAPTER TWENTY-ONE

Leona

Leona glanced around the cafeteria until she spotted her. She had thought all morning of why Cicily could be at Capmed, but the more she thought about it, the more anxious she became. Whenever Leona saw her, she immediately had to dismiss her to get to work. Luckily, Cicily didn't make a scene and accepted that they would have to wait until lunchtime.

But now, Leona would have preferred to push this inevitable conversation back another day or two. In fact, if she never had to face Cicily again, she would have been fine with that. She thought she had gotten her point across when she had spoken to her on the phone. Yet, there she was.

Cicily looked up when Leona approached her. "Should we grab our food first?" Leona muttered.

"Oh, sure." They dispersed, Leona heading toward the salads and Cicily toward the sandwiches. Once they both had their food, they paid and headed back to the same table where Cicily had been waiting for Leona.

"This is a nice hospital," Cicily began. "Nice cafeteria. When you think of New York, you'd think they would have all the higher tech and stuff and that Chicago would—"

"Be some Podunk little village?" Leona asked.

Cicily's eyes narrowed, and she looked down at her sandwich, then shook her head. "That's not what I meant or tried to imply." She grabbed her sandwich and took a bite, her eyes still down at the table.

Leona sighed. "I'm sorry. I shouldn't have just assumed that. I guess I'm a little on edge and maybe even a bit nervous. If I get snarky, I'll try to reel myself back in."

Cicily smiled and looked up. "You weren't being snarky. I can see how it would have come across that way, but Capmed is nice. That's all. And you even look happy here."

Leona raised an eyebrow. "You can tell I'm happy despite me being on edge?"

Cicily smiled sadly. "Of course I can tell. We were together long enough, and I can see it on your face. Besides, if you weren't happy, you might have considered coming back to New York."

"Doubtful," Leona mumbled. Leona met Cicily's gaze, seeing tears in her former lover's eyes. "I'm saying all the wrong things, aren't I?"

"You have every right to say what's in your heart." Cicily sniffled and looked away. The table grew quiet, and Leona considered getting up and just leaving. There wasn't anything Cicily could say that would bring Leona comfort. They had said all they needed to say when Leona had left New York, so why was Cicily there? Did she think that she could show up and everything would just magically change between them? Life didn't work like that.

After several minutes of neither of them speaking and only

shooting anxious gazes at each other, Leona broke the silence. "I'm not sure why you're here, but I guess I'll start the conversation."

Cicily held up her hand. "No, please. Let me. We left things on an uneasy note in New York. And that's mainly my fault, but I have been trying to pave a way where we could get back in each other's good graces. I miss you, Leona. I miss you as my girlfriend, but most importantly, I miss you as my friend. We used to be able to tell each other everything. When you left, that all changed."

"When you lied to me, that all changed."

Cicily sighed. "You're right. I lied to you. I made you think I wanted to be a mother someday. I knew that would tear us apart, so I misled you. I'm sorry, but at least the truth came out."

"After I got my hopes up," Leona shot back.

Cicily sunk back in her chair. "After you got your hopes up. I apologized then and I'll apologize now. It was awful of me. I'm sorry. Will you ever forgive me?"

"Cicily, I've told you I've forgiven you. And coming to Capmed was on a whim, but I *am* happy here. I've even met someone." Cicily lifted her eyes to Leona. "I'm happy. We're happy. We're slowly getting to a great place. But that's not even the half of it. I have a foster kid."

"You what?" Cicily gawked at Leona, disbelief written all over her face. Leona smiled, thinking about Brad. She quickly pulled out her phone to share a picture.

"He's six and I love the little guy. And so does Bella."

"Bella? The woman you're with?" Leona nodded.

Cicily stared at the picture for a long time. Finally, she smiled. "He's adorable."

"I can picture my life with this woman and with Brad. I can picture us being a family." She pocketed her phone and lifted her gaze. "If you don't want a child, then you should be with someone who shares those same beliefs. I would have never been able to be that person for you. That's why I was frustrated with the lies. I wanted us to start a family, and when the truth came out, I felt betrayed by you. I didn't have any ill feelings for you. I just wished you would have been honest with me before I planned out this perfect life for us."

"You're right. I really should have been. And I'm happy for you, Leona, especially if this all works out."

The two smiled tentatively at each other, and Cicily took a bite of her sandwich while Leona dug more into her salad.

"Tell me about her," Cicily said, breaking the walls completely down. Leona smiled, ready to share everything about Bella and happy that Cicily understood that they were never meant to be.

CHAPTER TWENTY-TWO

Bella

The elevator doors opened, and Bella went down the hall to Leona's office. She wasn't working that day, but she knew Leona was on shift, and she was anxious to see her. After her rough morning with her professor, seeing Leona's beautiful face would surely brighten her mood.

She peeked her head in her office, but Leona wasn't there.

She turned and saw Jacqueline headed out of a room. "Hey, Jacqueline. Do you know where Dr. Guillano is?"

"She's on lunch. She should be done in fifteen minutes or so, but she's down in the cafeteria."

"Thanks!" She waved and then got back into the elevator and took it down to the main floor. The first thing she wanted to do when she saw Leona was plant a passionate kiss on her. She could already imagine the way her body would react.

She stepped into the cafeteria and looked around. There weren't too many people milling around, so it wouldn't have been too difficult to find her in the barely-there crowd, but she scanned her eyes over every table, unable to spot Leona. She frowned and turned around, leaving.

It was possible they could have missed each other from taking the elevator—after all, there were two elevators—but not probable. Bella headed back to the elevator and pressed the button when she spotted Leona in the main lobby.

There you are. She started heading in Leona's way, but then slowed her steps to a complete halt. Leona was with another woman. Bella watched them embrace. It wasn't a friendly hug; there was some intimacy there. When the woman pulled away, she leaned in and gave a peck on Leona's lips.

Bella felt her eyes clouding over with tears. The two of them practically needed to get a room. She looked away, but then forced herself to look back. Leona stood there watching as the woman left through the front door. Bella swallowed the lump in her throat and turned away, then quickly maneuvered her way through the hallways until she reached Margo's office.

She didn't hesitate before she knocked.

"Come in!"

Bella practically burst through the door and Margo looked at her in surprise. "Bella? Did we have an appointment?"

Bella shook her head. "No, and I'm sorry for bursting in like this, but I just came from school. I'm not doing well in my classes and it's possible I could not graduate at the end of the semester if I don't change some things. Unfortunately, I feel it's in my best interest to drop out of the program."

"What?" Margo stood up and gawked at Bella. "Are you sure?"

Bella nodded. "I know it puts everyone in a bind, but I see no other way. If my grades fail, I'm out anyway. I have to do this for me. I hope you understand." She swallowed the lump in her throat. "I hope everyone understands." She grabbed a chair, afraid she was going to fall if she didn't have something to hold on to.

"Of course we understand. You have to do what's in your best interest. We'll all miss you, of course, but we know that you wouldn't do this if there were any other options."

There weren't any other options. Bella couldn't fathom running into Leona, or working with her when she knew that Leona had another woman on the side. Where did she even meet this woman? It didn't even matter. She couldn't let Leona see how much this hurt her. Bella had just opened herself up to life's possibilities with a hopeful heart, and now everything was crumbling.

"I'm sorry," she said again before leaving the room, about to burst into tears. She ran out of the hospital, fearful anyone would see how upset she was. And what was even worse, she didn't know if she was more upset because she had just dropped out of the program, or because of the fact that she had seen Leona making out with another woman. Who was she kidding? She knew exactly what upset her more.

When Bella got to her car and collapsed in her front seat, she couldn't stop the tears from flowing. How had her most promising semester turned into a total nightmare? She took time to dry her tears and then started her car and backed out of the parking spot. She was already emotionally unstable, but she had one more thing to do, and there wasn't any reason to stop herself now.

———

THE BELL DINGED AT THE JEWELRY STORE AS BELLA ENTERED. It was nearly empty, with only one woman browsing. Bella turned her attention to the desk, where both Jackson and an employee stood, chatting. Jackson looked up as Bella approached and gave a weak smile.

"Excuse me," he whispered to the employee, then walked around the counter and came to Bella. "Hello."

"Hello. Do you have a moment for us to go somewhere and talk?"

He nodded and reached for Bella's hand, walking her outside the store and to a quiet path. They had taken that path many times before, when they wanted to discuss life and the prospects of coming together as a family someday. But now, it felt like the place where they were going to be torn apart, and Bella knew neither one of them was at fault. She just hoped he saw it that way.

"It's a beautiful day today," Jackson said as they settled into a stroll around the block.

"That it is," Bella quietly replied. But they both knew she wasn't there to discuss the weather. And the sooner she got this out, the more at ease she would feel. "I want to start by saying you know how much I care for you, Jackson. Don't you?"

He chuckled. "No great conversation ever starts that way. But, in my heart, I really do."

"Right," she whispered. She just needed to say that. It was how she felt at that moment, and it was something that brought her purpose. "Work and school have rewired my brain. They've left me exhausted and with little time to spend with you. Half the time they made me wonder if I wanted to continue the nursing path, or just go out into the world and get a job in retail. I've been forced to think a lot about my life and what I really want."

Jackson let out a soft chuckle. "Coming from a guy that works retail, I would say that it isn't all that great, either."

"Well, perhaps it wouldn't have pulled me away from you. I curse everything that has kept us apart, because ultimately, it pushed me in another direction. Toward another person."

Bella stopped walking and Jackson slowed until he faced her directly. "Jackson, I didn't go looking to meet someone else. I just wanted to do my job and be happy with that. But I was working long and late hours at the hospital, and there was someone there that I couldn't help but get to know. And I knew that wasn't fair to you, so that's why I asked for the break. I needed time to think everything over."

"I see," he whispered.

"It wasn't something I had ever planned. I thought we would have a great life together, but this person…It was like she knew me better than I knew myself."

"She?" he asked, his jaw dropping.

Bella blushed and looked down at the ground, nodding slowly. Even though Bella realized after seeing Leona kiss another woman that Leona wasn't the woman she could be with, she couldn't deny that Leona had pulled her in a different direction, and she had to tell Jackson.

"Dr. Guillano, the woman I was on rotations with. She made everything exciting. We were constantly together, and it was hard not to find some sort of solace in her arms. And I'm so sorry that I didn't come to you first." She felt the tears stinging her eyes and before she knew it, she had started sobbing. Jackson pulled her into his arms and held her as she wept.

"Shhhhhh, don't cry," he whispered. As he held her, Bella slowly began to relax, then parted from his embrace. His eyes were light and not hollow, which wasn't what she had expected.

"I felt you pulling away, probably even before you were. I was sad that we could never see each other. And the truth is, I turned to someone myself. I didn't cheat on you, I promise. I met her recently, just after you started at Capmed. That's why I kept insisting we see each other. I was confused, too. I guess we were both meant to be with other people in the end."

"Is that who you went on vacation with?" Bella asked. He

tilted his head in confusion. "I came here and Nelly said you were out of town or something."

He sighed. "I needed some time away to think. I never did anything with this person, but she was someone I could talk to. I found myself getting too comfortable with her, especially since she's one of my employees. When I saw that it had gotten to that point, I realized the break you asked for was a good thing. Sorry I got a little desperate there and freaked out. That night you didn't answer my calls, I realized I needed to clear my head. I had to give us space to see what I wanted, too. I knew I needed to talk with you and see where your heart was." He shrugged. "And now I know."

"I never wanted to hurt you," Bella began.

"Or I, you." Jackson reached out and touched her arm. "Sometimes people just drift apart. It isn't anyone's fault, but more the fault of the universe. I don't blame you for this. I only want you to be happy."

"I only want you to be happy, too."

He pulled her back into his arms, and in that moment, Bella knew that whatever happened, they would both be okay. But right now, her heart was broken over losing not only Jackson but also Leona.

Grab your full copy of Melody in Her Heart now!

https://BookHip.com/LJDAWWT

"What Do You Do If Your Mind Can't Understand But Your Heart Can't Let Go?"

CHAPTER TWENTY-THREE

Leona

L eona exited a room and nearly bumped into Jacqueline, who was headed in the opposite direction. "Haley needs her meds," she said.

Jacqueline shook her head. "What'd you say?"

Leona frowned, tilting her head. "Haley Greene needs her meds."

Jacqueline had been known to be a bit flaky when it came to her work, but was acting flightier than usual. Her face was twisted and her eyes were nervously darting around. "Are you okay? You look like you could pass out. Or like you saw a ghost. Do you need to sit down or something?"

"No, I'm fine." She moved closer, closing the gap between them. "I just heard the news. I'm shocked. Like, I'm surprised I'm still standing. If anyone was going to jump ship, I thought it would have been..." She snapped her mouth shut and shrugged. "It's just so confusing, and she was doing well, too, right?"

Leona stepped back. "It would help if I knew what you were talking about."

Leona wasn't the type to get caught up in gossip, which Jacqueline seemed to be full of. She crossed her arms and arched her brow. If she waited any longer for Jacqueline to say something, she'd start tapping her food.

"You haven't heard?" Jacqueline's jaw dropped.

"Maybe I have, but I'm not sure what you're referring to, so it's really hard to know for certain. What is it?"

"Bella," Jacqueline said matter-of-factly. "She dropped from the program."

Leona laughed and shook her head. "Nope. I would know if she had. You're wrong."

She started to turn, but hesitated and looked over to Jacqueline, who was still standing there. "What makes you think that?"

"Just heard from Tori. She asked me to take some of Bella's shifts." She shrugged. "Pretty certain it's for real." She slowly backed away from Leona. "I should get to Haley's meds." She turned on her heel and hurried toward the medicine dispenser.

Leona looked over to the reception desk, where Tori sat, flipping through a folder. If it was true, she needed to get it straight from Tori, but she still hoped that Jacqueline didn't know what she was talking about.

"Tori!"

Tori looked up and gave a weak smile. "I'm doing everything I can to get these spots filled. I'm thinking we might have to shift some people around in the hospital. It could definitely work." She groaned. "Who would have thought, though?"

"So, it's true..." Leona's face fell. Why would Bella run off like this? It seemed to be a bad habit she had. When the going got tough, she got going. But for once, she had felt like they were in a great place. So why now?

"Yeah, I'm sorry. I thought the board told you or something." Tori scrunched up her face. "I didn't expect to be the one. I swore they said they would let you know."

"It's not your fault. But when? Do we know why?"

She shrugged. "Guess it got to be too much. It happened about two hours ago. But don't you worry. I'll do everything I can to make sure these shifts are filled before I leave today. You have my word."

"I have no doubt you will." Leona looked at her watch. "I'll headed out here in a bit. I have to get Brad from school, but I asked Many in ICU to cover me until I can get back."

"Sounds good. See you then." Tori looked back down at the folder and shook her head as she tried to figure out the new schedules.

If the staff didn't know the whole reason behind why Bella left, then Leona knew what she had to do. She had to get it straight from the woman Bella would have needed to speak with to drop out of the program.

She took the elevator to the main floor and headed straight for Margo's office. Luckily, the door was wide open, and Margo was working at her computer. When Leona knocked, she looked up.

"Guessing you heard," she said in greeting.

"I heard from Tori and Jacqueline, but now I want to hear it from you. Bella was doing well. Do you know why she decided to drop from the program?"

Margo sat back in her chair and sighed tiredly. "Unfortunately, some people just don't make it. I'll be honest. I thought Bella was different, but she said she felt it was too much for her given her coursework, and her grades were dropping. I can respect that. And we can only wish her the best." She leaned forward and grabbed a piece of paper from her desk. "With that being said, I wish she hadn't run out of here in the manner she did."

"She ran out of here?" Leona asked, confused.

She nodded and held up a piece of paper. "And I still need her signature. Without it, her decision to drop from the program can't be abided by. We need the form to be completed for it to be official."

"So, are you saying that if she came back and changed her mind, she would still be in the program?"

"Technically," Margo responded, her eyebrows raised.

"So, she would be welcomed back if she wanted to continue working here?"

Margo stared at Leona. "Do you think you could get her back? I mean, I'm all about second chances. If she just needed a break, a few days off, I could work with that. And until this paper is filled out, she still has a job. If you think you can convince her to change her mind, then good luck."

It was a long shot, but Leona was willing to try. She thanked Margo, then left her office and hurried toward the front door. She only had a little bit of time to get to Brad's school.

She already knew the conversation she would have with Bella once she was able to talk to her, and she knew she was going to speak from her heart.

————

"WHO ARE YOU HERE TO PICK UP?" THE WOMAN ASKED, looking down at a clipboard as Leona approached the beginning of the line.

"Brad Carver."

The woman looked up and frowned. "He's already been picked up."

"What?" Leona asked, staring at her. "That's not possible? By whom? When?"

The woman glanced around. "Thirty seconds ago. You just missed her. She said that you expected her to, and she was on the list." She turned and looked over her shoulder. "Shana!"

A younger woman hurried up to them. "Yeah?"

"That woman who picked up Brad, what was her name? You checked the list, right?"

She nodded. "Bella Strong or something like that. I can go look." She started to turn away, but Leona put up a hand to stop her.

"No need. In the rush to get here, it completely escaped my mind that I had asked her to get him." Leona smacked her forehead. "Silly me. Thank you, ladies."

She pulled away from the curb and hurried to return to the hospital, hoping she'd be able to catch Bella before she left from dropping Brad off at the day care.

The fact that Bella had still picked up Brad was a sign that Bella hadn't quit on account of Leona. It would have hurt Leona if she was the reason Bella felt she had to leave, especially when they were getting closer. But still, it didn't make sense why Bella didn't think of saying something to her, unless she planned on doing so once they were alone together.

Leona felt like she would never get back to the hospital. She kept imagining Bella getting further and further away from her. Finally, she pulled into the parking lot and made her way to her parking spot. Just a few more steps and she would be there. She rounded the corner of the day care and saw Bella coming out of the room.

Bella looked up and met Leona's gaze. "Hey," Leona said.

"Hey," Bella replied quietly. "I just got Brad settled in there."

"I forgot I had asked you to get him and I showed up at the school. They told me someone had already picked him up, and I about had a heart attack."

"Oh…I'm sorry. But it's all taken care of." Bella started to brush past her, but Leona reached out and touched her arm.

"Are you going to explain why you dropped from the program? You were doing so great."

Bella sighed and looked at her, Leona's hand still grasped on her arm. "Looks can be deceiving, I suppose. Just too much going on, I guess."

"But you didn't even tell me. Guess that hurt a bit."

Bella looked away. "It didn't look like we were sharing everything with each other."

"What's that supposed to mean?"

Bella glared at her. "I saw you, Leona. I saw you with that woman. And maybe I have absolutely no reason to be upset with you. After all, we never defined our relationship. I guess I was just foolish to think that we were exclusive or something."

"What? You've got this all wrong. The woman you saw was Cicily, my ex. I left her in New York when we realized that we weren't meant to be together. She didn't want a family, but she lied to me about it, stringing me along. She showed up here out of the blue. I had lunch with her, and we talked about it. I finally feel closure, and she feels at peace. When she left the hospital, we said our goodbyes, but that was it."

Bella stared at Leona. "Are you serious?"

Leona nodded and reached for Bella's arm, pulling her closer to her. "Is that why you dropped out of the program?"

Bella shifted her gaze to the floor. "Maybe it was part of the reason."

"Bella, you should have talked to me." She reached up and touched Bella's chin, guiding her eyes back to her. "I would have explained everything. And I had every intention of explaining everything once we saw each other."

"I was scared to learn the truth," Bella said softly.

"Well, we need to change that. You can't be scared any longer. Because I love you."

A smile crept on Bella's lips. "I love you, too."

Leona pulled Bella to her, and in the middle of the hall, she kissed her. They could figure out getting Bella back in the program later. For now, she just wanted to focus on Bella, the woman she loved.

EPILOGUE

Bella

Bella looked out to the audience and scanned her eyes over the crowd. She smiled when she saw her family sitting in a row together. Leona and Brad were seated right next to her mom and dad, and on the other side of her sister sat her brother and Jackson. She had never expected her life to take such a turn, but her heart was full.

"As every one of these students will tell you, it wasn't easy getting to this point, but I would hope by now, every single one of them would say it was well worth it. This class deserves all of your applause."

The crowd erupted into applause, and Bella glanced over at Professor Finch, who met her eyes. She knew that his words were most likely directed at her, but she felt excited about the future and grateful that she had made it past some pretty rough moments. She'd spent so much time thinking that if her plan didn't work out then her life would be ruined, and she'd be a failure. But that wasn't the truth. The truth was that sometimes, plans changed. Sometimes you had to release control and go with the flow and, like Leona told her, allow life to give you what you actually needed, what would really fulfill you and bring excitement to each day.

When the applause died, Professor Finch started rattling off names as the students walked up to grab their diploma. Bella was anxious for that moment when she would be able to walk through the stage and finally get her diploma. It felt like forever, though.

As she waited, she looked back to Leona and Brad. Brad was frantically waving at her, which brought a huge smile to her lips. She put her hand up and gave a slight wave.

Leona was beaming at her, and Bella was so caught up in staring at Leona's radiant smile that she nearly missed her name being called.

"Bella Strong!"

She looked up and caught Professor Finch smirking in her direction. She jumped up and quickly walked up to him.

"Congratulations, Ms. Strong."

"Thank you, Professor Finch." She turned her tassel and looked out toward her family, who were cheering and on their feet. She turned and went back to her seat and stared down at her diploma. Professor Finch's words came back to her from the day she'd turned in her extra credit. *Do you know why I'm so hard on you? I see great things in you, Ms. Strong. I know I appear difficult, but know that it's only because I believe in you.*

It was those words that made all the difference to her. In the end, Professor Finch had made Bella truly believe she was able to do it. Well, him and Leona. She smiled, thinking about her lover, and looked back out at the audience. Leona threw her a kiss and then winked at her. Leona's love was something she never thought she deserved, but now that she had it, she would do everything in her power to hold tight and never let go.

"Everyone, please give another round of applause for these graduates." As the crowd applauded, the graduates stood up and bowed.

Bella had made it. She left the stage with her fellow graduates and hurried toward where her family was—all of them, including Leona and Brad.

"Congratulations!" her dad said. She grabbed a hug from her each of her parents and her sister, then turned to Jackson.

"Thank you so much for coming, Jackson," she said, hugging him.

"Congratulations. You did it!"

She smiled and pulled back, then turned to Leona and Brad. She wrapped her arms around them, pulling them both into a hug. "I'm so proud of you," Leona said.

"Thank you." She moved in and kissed Leona, feeling that spark every time they were passionate with one another. "I love you."

"I love you."

Leona pulled her into another drawn-out kiss, and then Bella slowly pulled away. The end to her schooling had come, but her future was only getting brighter. She had gotten back in the nursing program at Capmed with just one nod of Margo's head, as if nothing had even happened. And now, she had been brought on as a full-time nurse.

Unfortunately, not everyone had made the cut, and Jacqueline had been transferred to a much smaller hospital. But Bella knew that it was Leona's recommendation that had secured Bella's spot at Capmed. However, as word got out about their relationship, they decided it would be best to work in different departments. Leona took the change in assignment, believing that Bella shined as a pediatric nurse.

"Can we go somewhere to talk?" Leona whispered. "Alone?"

Bella nodded and turned to her mom. "Will you watch Brad for a second?"

"Our pleasure."

Since Leona had fully signed the paperwork to adopt Brad a month earlier, Brad had become like a grandchild to Bella's parents. He was a part of their whole family.

Leona grabbed Bella's hand, and they walked away from the group. When they were in a secluded part of the auditorium, Leona turned to her. "Bella, things have been great between us. I love you. You love me. You love Brad. And I adore your family."

She laughed, slightly nervous. Bella saw her uneasiness as she shifted from one foot to the other.

"Leona, you don't let anything worry you, yet you seem so hesitant. What's wrong, my love?"

Leona relaxed and grinned at Bella's words. "Nothing's wrong. Everything is right—so right. I just want that feeling to always continue."

Leona took a breath and steeled herself. "Bella, you are the love of my life, and I…Well, I got you a very special graduation gift. Frankly, I can't stand the thought of waiting any longer. I spoke to your parents and your dad gave me his blessing."

Leona reached into her pocket and got down on one knee. "Bella Amelia Strong, will you marry me?"

How could one day get any more perfect? Bella had dreamed of those words so many times, and to be coming from Leona? She was overjoyed with emotion. She nodded eagerly. "I love you so much, Leona. Yes…I'll marry you."

Leona slipped the ring onto Bella's finger and then jumped up, pulling Bella into her arms. It was a happily-ever-after-ending to their story, and they both looked forward to the next chapter of their love.

COUNTING ON YOU!

A big thank you for trusting my book with your time, attention, and support. Here are two points to remember about reader comments (aka, book reviews):

1. I read all reader comments, so I can fix any errors and make my next book even better. *"Get busy polishing or get busy rusting,"* is my motto as a writer.
2. Imagine a sad world where readers are punished for dropping reviews. Whew! Fortunately, we have a better world, and you are the right writer to write right about this book. Please drop your honest opinions here:

https://www.amazon.com/review/create-review?ASIN=
B0BBL17FY4

or click on the QR Code below:

That would make my day! Thank you!

Happy Reading,
Morgan

P.S: Thanks, www.kindlepreneur.com, for the QR code generator:

https://kindlepreneur.com/qr-code-generator-for-authors

ABOUT THE AUTHOR

Morgan Cassen
WITH ROXIE

Morgan Cassen writes Lesbian Romance. Her mission is to make the world safer for sapphic stories to be told. Yes, she knows that there are millions of romance writers and billions of romance novels. So, why would she even think of adding to the pile? Well, Morgan has seen enough to know that the truly interesting stories are not what happen between human beings. That gig can seem pretty tame. At least compared to its older, tempestuous sister. Let's bring out Ms. Inner Conflict, the queen of all drama in the human world -- the ruler of the emotional map. Yes, the conflict between everything you've worked for and everything you want. You never imagined that all your hard work would put you so far away from everything you wanted. Also, how about the conflict between the past and the future? Being true to the past would require you to keep the future so far away in the future. But, how long can you postpone the future? What if your whole framing of the past can't stand the scrutiny of thoughtful analysis today even as you resolutely push the future away? Huh, what do you do with that kind of conflict? The conflict between human beings can look so tame compared to the real thing: conflict between you and you. You are the hero and villain at the same time, but the problem is that the villain thinks she is the hero, while the hero is all caught up in doubt. Which you will you choose? No, nobody else will make that choice for you. You get to make that choice, and your comforting, trusty friend--procrastination--can't seem to do the trick this time. The time has come for you to choose. See, inner conflict is where it's at. Inner conflict is what Morgan writes about in her books. Please join her as she writes the stories of breakup and love that tug at heartstrings.

Morgan is indebted to Sarah Wu (copyeditor) and Dr. Peter Palmieri and Nurse Karen Stockdale (medical advisors) for their extraordinary work and diligence. This book is so much better because of their efforts.

Stalk the author using the link below:

www.mtcassen.com

ABOUT PETER PALMIERI
(MEDICAL ADVISOR)

Peter Palmieri, M.D., M.B.A. is a licensed physician with over 20 years of practice experience in Chicago, Dallas, Houston, and the Rio Grande Valley in Texas. He received his B.A. from the University of California San Diego, with a double major in Animal Physiology and Psychology. He earned his medical degree from Loyola University Stritch School of Medicine and a Healthcare M.B.A. from The George Washington University. He is a regular contributor of original articles to a variety of health and wellness blogs.

ABOUT KAREN STOCKDALE
(MEDICAL ADVISOR)

Karen Stockdale, MBA, BSN, RN is an experienced nurse in the fields of cardiology and medical/surgical nursing. She has also worked as a nurse manager, hospital quality and safety administrator, and quality consultant. She obtained her ASN-RN in 2003 and her BSN in 2012 from Southwest Baptist University.  Karen completed an MBA in Healthcare Management in 2017. She currently writes for several healthcare and tech blogs and whitepapers, as well as developing continuing education courses for nurses.

ABOUT SARAH WU
(COPYEDITOR)

Sarah was born and raised in the concrete jungle of NYC. She loves traveling, exploring different foods, and giving the occasional tree a big hug. When Sarah isn't polishing up manuscripts, she enjoys spending time with loved ones and lovingly but firmly heckling them to decrease their plastic consumption.